# PRAYED UP

# PRAYED UP

### STEPHANIE PERRY MOORE

Dafina KTeen Books
KENSINGTON PUBLISHING CORP.
http://www.kensingtonbooks.com

DAFINA KTEEN BOOKS are published by

Kensington Publishing Corp.
119 West 40th Street
New York, NY 10018

ISBN-13: 978-0-7582-2538-2
ISBN-10: 0-7582-2538-5

First Printing: March 2008
10  9  8  7  6  5  4  3

Printed in the United States of America

*For Eugene Seals and Matthew Parker*
*(the two Michigan men who gave me*
*my first break in publishing)*

*I remember praying the Lord would send*
*someone to help me get my books in print!*
*Thanks to you both for answering His call.*
*Your heart to help others has blessed me.*
*I hope I'm being a good steward of what*
*you took a chance on.*

# Acknowledgments

When I was young, I never realized the power of prayer. Now that I'm older, I understand that praying to the Lord unlocks the door to anything I could ever need or want. If I feel sad, I could ask the Lord to lift me. If I'm confused, I could ask the Lord for direction. And when I'm mad, I ask Him to give me a sweet spirit. I pray now that this title helps each reader know that if they bow down they can be lifted up out of any situation, crisis, or dilemma.

See, prayer changes things. Though I will admit the Lord may not answer when you want Him to, I will say He is always on time. When you're feeling good, praise Him. When you feel sad, cry to Him. And when you're unsure, go to Him for direction. He will see you through. Here is a shout out to my prayer warriors.

To my family: parents, Dr. Franklin and Shirley Perry, Sr.; brother, Dennis and sister-in-law, Leslie; my mother-in-law, Ms. Ann; the Perrys; the Roundtrees; the Lundys and the Bradleys; I feel your prayers guiding me through. Your support is something I count on. Thanks for always being by my side, and for doing all you can to spread the word about my books.

To my publisher, Kensington/Dafina Books, and especially my publicist, Adeola Saul, your prayers really get me to the next level. I am thankful that together we can reach our young people. May Kensington continue being a house that cares about making a difference.

For my writing team, Antonio London Sr., Calvin Johnson, James Johnson, Ciara Roundtree, Jessica Phillips, Randy Roberts, Jason Spelling, Ron Whitehurst, Vanessa Davis Griggs, Larry Spurill, John Rainey, and Teri Anton, your prayers fixed a broken part of me. Your willingness to serve is huge. May the Lord bless you ten-fold for all you've done for this project.

To the special young men in my life: Leon Thomas (son), Franklin Perry III (nephew), Kadarius Moore (nephew), Dakari Jones (god son), Dorian Lee (god son), and Danton Lynn (god son), your prayers mean the world to me. Life may be tough for you at times, but in those moments, pray. The Lord is ready to listen and make your way smoother.

To my girlfriends' daughters: Donielle Dixon, Gloria Clark, Tatiana Bolds, Alexia & Ambrosia Floyd, Bryce & Brooke Bradley, Courtney Peace, and Hayli & Havyn Colon, your prayers give me wind to keep soaring. I hope this book helps you know God wants to talk to you always. Never forget that He is with you.

To my adorable daughters, Sydni and Sheldyn. Your prayers warm my heart. Remember, you can take all your worries to God. Like mommy, He is there to listen.

To my husband, Derrick Moore, your prayers complete me. Thanks for seeking the Lord for our family. It's good to have a best friend like you keeping me up.

To my readers, your prayers for my writing keep me going. Please take the principles within the pages to heart. God loves you and can make you whole.

And to my Savior Jesus Christ, your prayer to your Father on my behalf saved my soul. May the readers of this book bring you all their burdens. You make them light.

# Contents

# ~ 1 ~
# Going Over It

"Aw, Perry, please. Be for real. Of all four of us, you are the one with the least past drama. You are a goody-goody," Lance Shadrach said, as Deuce Avery and Collin Cox, my other two college roommates, laughed along with him.

It wasn't like the three of them were getting under my skin or anything, but I did sort of feel a need to defend myself. To most on the outside looking in, I had it going on. I had a physical body that most would kill for, and I now stood six feet four and a half inches tall. Weighing a thick, solid 225 pounds, I was strong. I could run faster than most on the team and leap almost as high as I was tall. That ability allowed me to catch balls that were uncatchable. As a freshman, without even playing a down, I had NFL scouts already calling my name. Though football had been good to me, it hadn't always been great. A lot of pressure and troubles come with the notoriety.

So I quickly said, "Don't y'all even try to forget, I didn't practice for most of the summer due to a recurring injury. What, y'all think it's easy to watch y'all get out there and do your thing?"

"Aw, come on, Perry," Deuce said. Deuce was also African American. He was a star running back and went to high school with Lance. Out of all the freshman players, he and I were the only ones who won a place on the first string. "I had to prove myself to get on Coach Red's list. You ain't really have to do all that. He signed you up to be his main man in the outfield right off the bat. You know you have it easier than all of us."

As I sat there watching the three of their mouths yap about me being some kind of privileged citizen or something, I wondered why in the world it even bothered me what they thought. I had always been a pretty confident guy, but at that moment, it was like I could see my self-esteem being zapped away with each word they spoke.

Immediately I defended myself. "Wait a minute. Have any one of y'all three chumps had a girlfriend tried to kill herself over y'all Negroes?"

"Is that politically correct, calling me a Negro?" Collin said in his proper and uptight voice.

Mr. Cox was the other white-boy suite mate. Collin was from Alabama. He's supposed to have a great leg to kick through the uprights, but he'd been a little inconsistent during the summer practices. The coach and the rest of the team were now skeptical that he'd be able to carry us in the event our first-string kicker could not play.

Lance picked up a pillow and bopped him on the head, "Man, he just playing. We're roommates; we're brothers in a sense. Haven't we got through the whole racial thing?"

"I was just asking," Collin said, looking like a teacher had reprimanded him.

"So back to my question—have any of you had that? Don't be looking all crazy," I said to them as their mouths shut at the same time.

They all drew closer to me to hear the details. Thinking back on the scary incident, I couldn't even believe the day I found Tori, my old girlfriend of three years, sitting in her car trying to OD on the toxins. If I hadn't gotten there and opened up the car door, who knows what would have happened to her. My point, of course, wasn't to brag that I was all that and that she had to go to such lengths because she had lost me, but the dudes were saying that I was drama-free. Certainly that incident alone would get them the heck off my back.

"Whatever, man, a little girlfriend problem ain't nothing that major. My girl got pregnant!" Deuce said. "And though she gave up the baby for adoption, it's not a week that goes by that I don't think about the child I fathered."

He had me. I remembered the pregnancy scare that happened to my homeboy Cole. Another one of my boys, Damarius, got an STD. I had to be with him through that. But it wasn't me. Though I was deeply affected, I wasn't even trying to plead my case like that.

"My best friend almost killed me," Lance admitted.

"What?" I said shocked.

Deuce chimed in, "Yeah, because he tried to take his girl. Lance is not a real loyal friend. You know that firsthand, Perry, don't you?"

I chuckled. I certainly did remember when I first got to college and Lance made moves on my new girl, Savoy. In his defense, technically she was fair game. Savoy and I weren't going together any longer because right before we came to college, I had broken her trust by sleeping with my former girl, Tori, the one who tried to kill herself because I had left her.

Yeah, I had a lot of issues going on. I used to get myself in deeper, deeper, and deeper. Now that I was in college, I wanted to make sure I did things the right way. It was time for me to grow up and carry less baggage around. I knew it was going to be hard enough to make it at Georgia Tech.

"But, have you ever been hemmed up by police?" Deuce asked me. "Probably not, because you aren't the average black man. Folks don't mess with Perry Skky Jr. You're royalty in this state."

I had to tell him about a few months back. "Aw, see, I was in Hilton Head . . ."

"Well, that explains whatever bull you were about to try to feed us. You weren't even in Georgia," Deuce said, as if cops in our state were the meanest jokers around.

"Naw, y'all gonna listen," I said, knowing that I was dealt with unfairly. "I see this cute girl on the beach late one night. She's crying and all, and I'm the only one out there. I was actually trying to catch up with the other players on the team who went to this little camp. Chaplain hooked it up for us. Thought it was going to be a vacation. Shoot . . . I go to help her, turns out she had been raped, and then these three white dudes come along. Bash my face, all assuming I'm the one that messed with her. Next thing I know, the cops jack me up without any interrogation. Finally the girl comes to and tells them it wasn't me. She was date raped. What's even more a trip, the girl goes to Tech. She's a freshman here, too."

"Ooh, small world," Deuce said.

"Yeah, if she was real cute, I need to meet her," Lance teased.

Quickly I told him, "Please, you aren't her type. I saw her last week, and she wants me."

Lance, Deuce, and I laughed and kept messing with each other. We wanted to find out which one of us was the toughest. All three of us thought we had had it the roughest. However, when Collin spoke, he had us all beat.

Collin said, "Have any of you ever wanted to take your own life?"

All jokes were put aside at that point. We didn't know whether he was playing or was serious. We didn't know what in the world he was talking about. We had no idea where that comment even came from, but it certainly made us stop and be serious for a moment.

All of a sudden, Lance broke the silence and said, "Nah, I've never wanted to do that."

Deuce said, "Nah, I ain't never want to do that either."

Something inside me made me ask, "Why, Collin? You've been there?"

Collin yelled, "Just forget it." He got up from our family room area and went into his own bedroom.

When he slammed the door, instantly I prayed aloud: "Lord, my boy Collin has issues. Actually, all three of us do. You know I didn't even want to open up. In Jesus's name I pray. Amen."

When I opened my eyes, I was surprised to hear Deuce say, "You talk to the Lord often? I need to do it more."

"Yeah, partner, I understand," I responded. "We need to stick to keeping each other accountable."

Deuce and I slapped hands.

Lance cut in and said, "Enough of the mushy stuff. Let's get ready for the big party. We're headed to the big national championship game. I can feel it. We might as well celebrate early."

"You really think we got a shot?" I asked him, doubting my own abilities to help lead a team to that type of victorious season.

Confidently, Lance replied, "If I get to start, then I'll guarantee it."

I so wanted his type of buoyancy. Looking back on all I'd been through the last year had really taken a toll on my psyche. However, that was all in the the past. I couldn't use my issues as a crutch. I was a college freshman. Time for me to walk positively and enjoy my life. I really hoped I could conquer my negative thinking.

\* \* \*

September in Georgia is usually hot, but this pre-autumn night was a sizzling ninety-seven degrees Fahrenheit. As if it wasn't enough to live with three crazy football players, across the hall was my girlfriend's twin brother, Saxon Lee. He had enough ego to match the whole football team. He was so proud to host the freshman bash. I wasn't into all the partying, but if you can't beat 'em, join 'em, right? And I knew the music would be blaring so loud that I wouldn't be able to get any sleep. So it didn't take much pushing by Deuce and Lance to get me to attend.

"Okay, why we got to be moving all of your furniture?" Lance said, ragging on Saxon and his defense-player room-mates, whom I didn't really know yet.

"You plan to eat all my chips and drink the punch I made. Shoot, I might as well get my money's worth out of y'all chumps. Plus I'm going to give you access to a bunch of hon-eys that are going to be in the house tonight," Saxon said be-fore walking over to me. "Now, Perry, I am just making sure you understand the only person *you* need to be caught within twenty feet of is my sister."

"Man, get your hands out of my face," I said to him as I shoved him back.

Breathing all in my space, Saxon said, "What? What you think? I ain't supposed to look out for my sister? I know you ain't right for her."

"Man, don't even insult me like that," I said, smelling the alcohol on his breath.

Deuce stepped in between the two of us and said to me, "Come on, man, you know Sax."

"Yeah, I do. The problem is, Sax don't know me."

"What's that supposed to mean, Perry? If any of y'all see him cheating on my sister and don't say any-anything, I am holding you just as much re-re-shon-pible as him."

"Alright, man, calm down. You're drunk," Deuce said as he pulled Saxon over to the corner.

Just when I was about to leave to cool off, I opened the door to a knock and had to play host. I couldn't count how many folks walked past me, but the apartment was instantly filled, and one thing Saxon was right about—the hotties were in the place. Women not just from Tech were there. He'd invited Spelman and Georgia State girls as well.

Three girls back-to-back asked me to dance. Showing Saxon that he didn't own or scare me, I obliged them all. Then, as I tried to find a corner to sit, Savoy stepped in my path, looking finer than a sharp razor blade.

"Ah, I think this next dance is mine," Savoy said, as she turned my chin toward her face and planted a juicy kiss on my lips.

Her brother could definitely never say he could tell me what to do. Plus there was nothing wrong with my eyes checking out the scenery. However, after that very wet exchange, clearly my heart thumped for his sister. He didn't have to worry.

We moved to the dance floor, and she placed my hands on her hips. We were in sync grooving to the music. Then a slow jam came on, and I was going to head off to get us a soda or something, but she made sure I didn't move. She tugged me in closer. To feel her chest up against mine made me want to get her in a room alone. My desire was rising.

"I thought about you all night last night," she whispered into my ear while our bodies continued to sway.

Her damp tongue let me know she was as attracted to me as I was to her. She'd been flirting all evening. We danced to five songs straight. As more and more people entered the room, there was less and less room to breathe. I had gotten my true groove on only once, though I had connected with my former girlfriend. I desperately wanted to be intimate with Savoy.

She was a track star, and for good reason: her body was chiseled and sexy. But she and I had vowed not to go there in our relationship. I wanted to honor what we said, yet at the same time, as her body moved to the left and the right, our pledge to pursue abstinence was becoming a distant memory.

"You said you've been thinking about me?" I said as I kissed her head and then let my tongue slide down her sweaty cheek. "Care to fill me in on the details?"

"Why tell you when I can show you?" She led me to the door. When we got outside, she said, "Your place is across, right? Let's go to your room."

"You sure you want to do that?" I said, standing in front of her. She took my hand and placed it right between her legs. Quickly, I found my keys and opened up the door, and our lips met as we made our way to my bedroom. She undressed me as I did the same to her. As we stood there completely bare, excitement grew between us.

"I want you so bad," she said. She came close to me, and our bodies began to sway together all on their own. I forgot about everything—my commitment to purity, thoughts of protection, and the complications intimacy may or may not bring to our relationship. We were in the heat of passion. There was no time to weigh the pros and the cons. It was put-out-and-enjoy time. Expressing how much I cared for her came naturally. She let out a sigh, and for the first time was one with a guy. At that moment, I honestly believed there was no way that what felt so right could be so wrong.

The next day, I was on a private jet with the team, headed to sunny California to play in our first ball game. The USC

Trojans were expected to beat us. A lot of hype surrounded the game. ESPN analysts were even broadcasting from the stadium.

I should have been focused on the route and scheme of the game, but all I could do was go over my previous night's actions. I remember it was six in the morning when Savoy rolled over and woke me. I never slept all night with a girl, and thought it felt great that our bodies were together under the covers. Then she said, "I love you." I was just messed up. It was a real awkward moment between us because she was waiting on me to say it back to her. I couldn't say the words because I wasn't sure. I knew I was committed to being with her alone, but love? Dang! We'd parted with much distance between us.

"Hello," the stewardess said, interrupting my thoughts. "Can I get you something to drink, sir?"

That was about the fifth time someone had come up and down the aisle offering something. I don't know what I expected these charter flights to be like, but it was really an endless spread. They had huge hamburgers, grilled chicken sandwiches, chips, ice cream bars, candy bars, Gatorade, Coke, water, fruit, and chewing gum. While most of the team put on headsets to watch the movie shown during the flight, I grabbed my heart.

After our lovemaking was done, Savoy asked me if I'd pulled out in time. Heck, I was unsure. She had caught me off guard with that question. I thought I was cool, breaking myself away from her as I had my moment of pleasure, but now that she had asked the question, I prayed I didn't leave any unwanted specimen floating around.

"You on birth control?" I remember asking her.

"Why would I need that?" she answered.

Coach Red came down from his seat and said to me, "Alright, son, you got your head in the game? This is a big one. This will set us up for the big championship. I know you're ready, right?"

He hit me in the arm really hard. I just looked at him, though a part of me was very nervous about the first game, since I didn't want to let anyone down and all. I knew the answer he wanted to hear, so I said, "I'm ready, Coach."

"That's my boy!" he said.

Deuce and I roomed together on the road. My teammate and friend knew me very well.

"Alright, man, you've been moping around this room all night. What's up?" Deuce asked me the next morning.

"Probably just jet lag," I muttered.

"Don't give me that. Talk to me. What's up?"

"I don't know. Nationally televised game tonight, Deuce, I guess."

"Hey, man, everybody's a little nervous. We're all trying to take this team to the next level. It starts here. You'll be great."

"Thanks, man!" I said, not wanting a pep talk, but feeling better now that I had had one.

Later we had chapel. I was the first one there and planted my butt right in the first seat, ready to get a word. I needed to hear something to keep me calm. I had played in many games in my life. Even on the JV team, in the ninth game they upgraded me to varsity. I had always played with the big boys. I didn't understand why I was doubting myself.

"Well, hello, men."

"Hello," we all responded. The majority of the football team was present, hoping to get a charge from the chaplain.

"Listen, I don't need to get you ready for this game. I'm sure your adrenaline is flowing more than a race car's energy. Quite honestly, if you aren't already excited, with all the hype surrounding this season opener, then you aren't really a football player. They got a packed crowd out there tonight. You're gonna be on national TV—lights, camera, action. All eyes will be glued on you, so you should be ready and actually a little nervous. I will say this: In the midst of this hostile environment—a storm, so to speak—you have to know, you have to believe that God is on board. He will calm the storm."

I was really fired up after the chaplin's talk. After I was in my uniform, I knelt down and prayed: *Lord, I just need you to keep me focused on this game. I feel like my leg is a little too shaky and not fully healed from my injury. I just got too many doubts going on. Just help me through it. In Jesus's name, I pray. Amen.*

Mario, the team's quarterback, came up to me and said, "Look, man, I got a lot riding on this game."

The way he said it, I was a little skeptical. What did he mean? Quickly I dismissed the thought. I was too in my own world to ask him any questions.

"Alright, man, I'm gonna do my part."

"Now, that's what I'm talking about. No one thinks we can win this, but I can win big if we do. You know what I'm saying?" He hit me in the arm.

In the first quarter, we came out strong. We scored the first touchdown and silenced the garnet-and-gold crowd. My boy Deuce ran it in from five yards out.

"It's time to play some ball!" Coach Red said with enthusiasm on the sidelines.

But we knew as soon as their offense stepped on the field that we would clearly have our hands full. Their quarterback threw a forty-five-yard pass back to their wide receiver. He ran a slant and took it to the two-yard line. Our defense held them once, but on the second try, they scored. The ball game was tied going into the second quarter.

Coach Red talked to us before we went back out on the field. "Listen, men, this is what we practiced for. This is what we played for. This is a real game situation. *Are you ready?*"

The next quarter and a half, no one scored, but in the third quarter, the Trojans scored two field goals back-to-back.

"Alright, Perry, your number's up," Mario said as we got back into a huddle.

He threw the ball to me. I had been double-teamed the whole night, so found limited passes coming my way. Now they wanted me to step up. It was the fourth quarter and time was getting short. Just before the ball reached me, I tried to remember, "Did I pull myself away from Savoy in time?" What the heck was I thinking? I was in the middle of a ball game. The ball came right into my hands and I dropped it. Unfortunately, their defensive back caught it and ran it in for a touchdown. I just sank to the carpeted grass; I didn't even want to jog to the sidelines. But I had to suck it up and be a man. Nine times out of ten, I would have caught that ball. With not enough time on the clock for us to get another possession, our only hope was for our special team to run it in. That play went astray.

I was not the hero, but the zero of my team. Nobody said anything positive to me when I got to the sidelines. Looking up at the replay on the big screen in the stadium, I saw I had no excuse for not catching that ball.

Finally, Deuce came up to me and said, "Hey, man, don't sweat it. We'll get 'em again."

Angry, I huffed, "Like we'll play the Trojans again."

"Well, there ain't nothing you can do about this game, so quit going over it."

# ~ 2 ~

# Riding Out Storms

"I'm sorry, but I just don't feel up to it," I said to Marsha Cross, the sports information director for our school. "I just had a bad game. I can't talk to the press."

I guess I had forgotten what level I was playing at. I wasn't calling the shots. I was a highly recruited player, and the press wanted me to speak. I just wasn't ready to talk about it. I had no idea, however, that Coach Red was standing right behind me.

"Coach, he says he's not up to it," Ms. Cross said.

I couldn't be mad at her; this was her job. She was supposed to get the players the press wanted to interview to the podium to answer questions at the mic. I never understood why losing teams had to give interviews anyway.

Coach Red touched my arm and said, "He'll be there in just a second." He nodded, and then she turned and walked away. "Look here, I've seen your high school film. Pretty much every game you had was an A-plus performance. Notice how I said 'pretty much.' Every now and then, you made a stupid decision, but you got it together and made an impressive career. Back then, you may have been able to tuck your head in between your legs and go home, but on this level, it doesn't work like that, son."

"I understand, Coach," I said, mumbling what I thought he wanted to hear to get him off my back.

"No, you need to hear me out. You're one of the top freshmen in the country—"

"Not no more!" I said, feeling deflated.

"You keep that attitude and you'll be right. Your stock will never rise above this low performance thinking negatively. So put your head on and be a man. Take your medicine like you're supposed to. Be humble and win the reporters over. Take the blame before they can blame you, and let's move on. If we're going to get to the big dance at the end of this, you're going to be a big part of that."

"You think so?" I asked him, doubting myself once again.

"Yeah, I do. But during a game, you must stay focused. I've been coaching long enough to know that dropped passes like yours are probably due to a lack of concentration. Now, I don't know what was going through your mind when that ball went through your hands, but it was clear to me that your head wasn't in the game. Son, you need to shake this one off, talk to the media, get your butt on that plane, and get ready to go get 'em next week. You hear me?"

"Yes, sir."

"Then come on." Coach led the way through the news-hungry sports reporters.

Two hours later, I was so glad to be on the bus on the way to the airport and to get out of what was supposedly sunny California. That day, it was anything but sunny for me. I realized that Coach Red did know what he was talking about. All I had to do was not make excuses for my poor performance and the reporters backed off. Some said they couldn't wait to see me in the upcoming weeks. With that behind me, and my body still on Eastern Standard Time, I was so tired. All I wanted to do was get on the plane and sleep for the four-hour flight. Unfortunately, Lenard, the smart-mouthed wide receiver that covered the other side of the field, stepped up to me just after I checked my bag. The way he stared me down, I knew he was about to let me have his unsolicited thoughts. However, as we walked through the terminal, he was silent.

Once we boarded the plane, Lenard said, "I don't know why the media wanted to talk to your punk behind. Because of you, we lost the game."

I just looked at him and let my eyes roll.

"Oh, you can't talk now? You can't respond? I saw you during the interview. You had a whole lot to say then."

"Lenard, get out of my face." I took my hand and shoved him into a seat.

"Oh heck naw, it's on," he said, swinging at the air before a couple of other players pinned him down.

Deuce said to him, "Man, let's go."

I walked on by and went to use the john. Mario came up to me and said, "Hey, man, didn't I tell you I had a lot riding on this game? I threw the big pass your way because I just knew you were going to catch it, not give the game away, dang. You owe me, and I will be collecting."

Mario took his hand and punched me in the chest. I didn't know if this was some sort of hazing stuff because I went as a freshman or what. The last thing I needed was more strife with my teammates. I had just gotten into it with Lenard. I didn't need two of my offensive starters breathing down my neck. Then Marques Jackson, a senior linebacker, held his leg out in the middle of the aisle as I tried to go back to my seat.

"What's up, man?" I said with an attitude.

"You trying to get by? You trying to sit down? Dang, seats are only for those who work hard on the field. You might need to stand up the whole plane ride home."

It was one of those moments in my life when I didn't

know what to do. I mean, I didn't even know Marques; we ran in different circles. He was one of those brothers who was cool, but not my speed. He was operating in a whole other zone. I knew he was a bully. But I was no pushover. Besides, I had not taken it from Lenard. I hadn't taken it from Mario. So at the crossroads again, I didn't know if I could. I guess it showed on my face that I was anxious.

"Aw, don't cry now, freshman," he said, taunting me. "I need to take you to the club and let my women loosen you up."

Marques lowered his leg just enough and I stepped over it. I had no idea he'd be such a jerk and try to trip me up. Just my luck, my seat was right in front of his. We sat on the runway for an extra thirty minutes, which made matters worse. We were instructed by the tower to wait out a big storm that had brushed in. Finally, when we took off, I was ready to sleep, but as soon as we reached cruising altitude, the plane took a huge dip.

"Oh my gosh! Oh my gosh!" Marques squealed, showing which one of the two of us was the bigger baby.

Then the plane took a spiraling nosedive. I didn't know what was going on. All of us started hollering something or other. Was this the end for me? I could only silently pray: *Lord, I know I haven't been a great son, but I'm trying. If You get me out of this, I'll try to find a way to please You more.*

Deuce grabbed my forearm and shouted, "Aw, man. Oh Lord. Help us, God!"

I heard guys crying as the plane kept shaking. My stomach was dropping worse than on any rollercoaster that I had ever been on. Just when I thought it was over, just when I asked the Lord to remember me if this was it, the plane leveled out and started climbing.

The pilot came on the loudspeaker and said, "We're going

through a bad storm, as you can see, but it looks like we've gotten out of the bad pocket. Flying just a little bit under the lightning should help us for the rest of the flight and make it smooth sailing."

All of the hostility and frustration I had for some of my teammates was gone. It all seemed so trivial. After all, they had a reason and a right to be angry with me. If I knew I did my best and let them down, that was one thing. But I couldn't really be mad at them knowing deep within the real reason I dropped the ball was that I was unfocused. Now that I had been there and done that and seen the results of what thinking about other things during a football game can do, I was ready to not make that mistake anymore. I could only pray that this storm of distraction, like the storm the plane just went through, was over.

Monday nights at Tech, we had our Fellowship of Christian Athletes (FCA) praise rallies, led by the chaplin. I wasn't going to go. Tons of schoolwork was keeping me on my toes, and Sunday I had been worn out from the travel on Saturday, the horrible flight home, and watching the game tape of my play over and over again. If it wasn't on ESPN, it was on the local news, and then, of course, my position coach made me watch the film. It actually hurt double knowing I let the team down, and my coach didn't let me off easy. Coach Griggs was all in my face. But staying home wallowing wasn't going to help.

I had several messages on my cell phone. My parents had called four times. Savoy had called eight, and Damarius had hit me up a couple times. Everybody with the same thing: "Are you okay?" "Heard about the emergency landing." Our story had gotten changed. We didn't have an emergency landing, just a shaky plane ride. But I didn't feel like talking to anybody.

But then Deuce knocked on my door and asked, "Are you ready to go to the meeting?" Before I could respond, he said, "Ain't even no need to say you ain't going. Let's just give God His time and make this thing right."

As soon as we got outside the door, lightning struck and thunder started to roll. I wanted to use it as an excuse and say, "Hey, I'm just gonna stay in." But Deuce gave me a "you're not getting out of this" look.

Our apartment door opened again, and Lance came out and said, "Hey, y'all leaving me? I'm going to the meeting."

I rolled with the two of them in Lance's hoopty. He was the coolest white boy I'd ever met. People could do what they wanted to do when they wanted to do it because, though it was raining elephants and gorillas, the players' lounge was packed. It was like every team on Tech's campus had at least five people in the room. About 150 people packed the place, making it pretty much at capacity.

Before I could sit down, Savoy touched my arm and said, "I don't understand. I've been calling you and calling. My brother said your plane ride was pretty bad. Also, I saw your play. I know you've got to be down, and you won't call me back, with all we've shared?"

I wanted to say, "Well, alright. Don't go there with me. Yes, we're close. You're my girl. But sometimes a man just needs space." I saw too many folks looking in our grills, though. So I kept quiet. I just sort of looked at her. I wasn't on drugs or anything, but I certainly appeared as if I were in a daze. My eyes drifted up.

And she asked, "Why you got to roll your eyes at me? If you didn't want to talk to me, you could have just picked up the phone and said that. Tell me right now so I can get up and leave you alone."

I touched her elbow, pulled her to me, and whispered in

her ear, "We don't need to make a scene, Savoy. You just said I've been dealing with a lot. Cut me some slack, okay?"

"Alright, it's time to get started!" Chaplain Morris called out.

At first, I was a little bit apprehensive as the white guest with the guitar started to play some kind of praise song. Then when I looked at the words on the screen and the music became more familiar, I had no problem singing out to the Lord. I needed God to come fill my heart. It didn't matter that the musician had a Christian rock style. It was different from the gospel I was used to. I hated that I wasn't sure of myself. And it wasn't about having too little faith in God; it was about having too little faith in me. I didn't know how to reverse what I was feeling. But the song helped a bit.

The chaplain began, "Today I am going to talk about little becoming much. In the Bible, there is a story where God fed five thousand people two fish and five loaves of bread. We're at the beginning of a new school year. I was with the football team when we didn't get the win we wanted. And as cross-country and golf start up, I am here to motivate you guys today. Just as God took little and made much with it back then, He can do that today in your lives. I mean, let's face it, you're college athletes. A lot of pressure is on you to succeed athletically, as well as academically. Not to mention other drama you may have going on. I understand. I have been here for five years, and I remember my own college days. It takes a lot to stand for Christ daily, but I'm telling you today that you have what it takes to make Him proud. You are able to live a life that shows He rules and abides in your life."

I was trying to focus, but I could see Savoy suddenly looking at me every few seconds. It wasn't like I couldn't understand what she was feeling. I pulled away, and that left her feeling neglected. I had gotten myself in a pickle. Though I had wanted to be intimate with her then, now I had doubts, and our relationship was ill. I wasn't just a brother who tried to hit it and run, but for sure I wasn't a brother trying to get married and all that stuff either. What did she want from me, and what could I honestly give her?

Shucks, Savoy might even be pregnant. What in the world would I do with a kid? I didn't even want to ask her about any of that. I had my own issues concerning the football team to deal with.

We had a home game, our first of the season, coming up in fewer than seven days. Although we were playing a team we should be able to beat, Memphis had a program that was growing. It wasn't going to be a pushover. And with the little athletic ability that I had displayed this Saturday, would God be able to put me back on the field and do much? Could I take tonight's Bible lesson and really believe there could be a lesson there featuring me?

When the meeting was over, I told Savoy that I needed to talk to Chaplain Morris. She didn't like it, and she stalked off. I didn't go after her. Sometimes she just needed to deal with her own stuff.

We went to the chaplain's office, which was right off the big room. He shut his door and said, "Okay, so something's been up with you, boy. I was about to talk to you on the plane the other night, but I could tell from your demeanor that you just wanted space. Then, of course, the crazy plane ride sidetracked me. I figured you'd come to me. I'm glad you finally did. What's going on with you?"

"I don't know, Chaplain. I wish I did, but I feel different. It's like I'm letting God down in so many ways, it's spinning all out of control. It's like I have on shoes that are too big for me or something."

"Well, boy, you better get some shoestrings, lace them up, tie them tight, bow yourself up, and get ready to get back out on that field Saturday. I know that. Shake off the bugs. Everybody's not going to have a great game every time, not even the great Perry Skky. Put that game behind you; leave it behind you."

"Yeah, but if I let God down, you think He could punish me on the field?"

"God doesn't work like that, son. Yes, there are consequences to our actions. It seems like you have some mental stuff going on due to some of your choices. As cute as your girlfriend is, I probably have an inkling of what's going on. However, we can't change yesterday. We can only ask for forgiveness, and believe God will forgive us, and move on. There comes a point in time when you have to forgive yourself."

All of a sudden, the lightning and thunder stopped. I heard him, and maybe he had a point. What was done was done.

"Oh, that's good. Everyone can get home safely," Chaplain Morris broke in and said. "Just like this heavy rain stopped, you've got to believe that the hard times in your life will stop, too. You're on an emotional rollercoaster ride. Get through it, man. Like I said a minute ago, there is much in you. Believe it is there, and it will come out."

It was another Friday night, and the football team was nestled in a nearby hotel. Even before home games, the whole team was housed together to prevent distractions. Deuce and I were still roommates, and he had gone to get a snack. I looked at myself in the mirror in the fancy double room and felt bad that I hadn't talked to Savoy. I knew she cared for me in a real sincere way, and it wasn't fair that I had been missing from her world. The more and more I thought about it, the more I realized I didn't like her missing from mine. Even with all I had been going through, I was aware she had issues as well. It wasn't fair to her to assume she didn't need her man to talk to. As I called her, I braced myself for a well-deserved reprimand.

I was shocked when she said, "Hey, I didn't think I would hear from you! You okay?"

That was the Savoy I had fallen for. She wasn't demanding or high maintenance. She was the kind of girl who accepted everything for what it was. She was down to be there for me through the bad and the good. Her voice sounded so cool, so calm, so collected. I wanted to say "I miss you," but I held back those words from flowing from my mouth. Honestly, I refrained because I didn't want to give her a chance to cut in and say, "No, I shouldn't even be talking to you right now, you did me so wrong."

So to deal with the distance issue, I said, "I know I don't deserve you talking to me at all. I really have been a jerk, real selfish."

"That's alright," she said, cutting me off, surprising me yet again.

"I realized my tactics on Monday were a little abrasive. You didn't deserve that," I said sincerely, hoping that she would give me grace.

"Nah, I didn't. But Ray Charles could have seen you needed your space. A relationship is a two-way street. I don't have you in handcuffs, Perry, and I don't want to smother you. I know so many people are putting expectations on you, and I know it's got to be tough. Every time I turn on the TV or open the newspaper or hear a professor talk about the game, they're always excited about what the freshman wide receiver that every school in America wanted is going to do for our 'great Institute of Technology.' So, I'm not even kidding myself; I don't know how this thing between us will last. Just know that sometimes I'm a little menstrual."

"What do you mean?" I said, laughing, thinking about my

sister, Payton, taking up all the space in the cabinets in our connecting bathroom with all her women's products.

"That means that sometimes I have feelings I can't control, but I've been trying to pray and give this all to God. Let Him work out all the turmoil.. He's been calming me," Savoy explained. "I've been praying for you, too, asking God to give you peace. If we found our way back to each other, cool. If we didn't, how could I be mad at Him? He clearly laid out in his word what we should and should not do in a dating relationship, and I just let my hormones get the best of me."

"Well, I ain't going nowhere," I said, cutting in. "What's been going on with you?"

"Just trying to find my way. Not that many black girls around here. Being in a new place is never easy."

"But there's a lot of white boys," I teased, referring to her race preference before we dated. "I figure I need to act right, since you have a lot of options available."

We both laughed.

"Naw, I think I'm gonna be sticking with the brothers. One has completely turned me out."

"I'm sorry," I said, truly believing God makes a man accountable in a married relationship. I was to blame for not leading us the right way. "Are you okay, Savoy?"

"I am."

"Well, how about tomorrow after the game, win or lose, we talk?"

"I'd like that. Have you talked to your mom?"

"Why did you ask me that?" I questioned.

"I don't know. Something just tells me you shut out everybody who cares about you. I talked to Tad, and he said Payton said something like that. I feel led to tell you maybe you should call her too."

"You really do care about me, don't you?" I asked, understanding the depths of her feelings for me.

"You know I do," she said before we hung up the phone.

Finally not being a knucklehead, I dialed my mother's number.

"Son," my mom said into the receiver. "Baby, I've been so worried."

"I know, Mom."

"Baby, I know it's a lot of pressure on you!"

"Yep, sometimes it feels like I'm caught up in a tornado."

"Baby, I've been lifting you up to the Lord. Just do what you can. Don't let the rest of it stress you."

"Mom, I just don't want to let anybody down."

"Well, you know what they say when you're in the eye of the storm: That's really the safest place to be."

"I don't understand," I said.

"Block out all of the noise around you. Don't let the destruction weigh you down. You have the strength to succeed, to succeed in whatever the Lord has in store for you. It may or may not be to become a great college athlete. However, if that's what you want for yourself and God has equipped you with the skills, you just have to tap into all of it. Seize it."

"Yes, ma'am." I said. "I'm going to have a great game tomorrow."

"I know you will, baby."

Football was America's favorite game. It certainly was mine. I loved it because it was a team sport. Having my teammates back in my corner pumped me up even more.

Mario, the quarterback, came up to me and said, "Alright, look, rookie," which was a term he joked on because I was a freshman, "I know you're going to get out there and do your thing today. Shake off what happened before. Let's win this together."

More and more players came to me as I strapped on my pads. Their kind words made me want to achieve. I was ready.

Unfortunately, we had to wait an extra hour for kickoff because of a severe storm, but once that was cleared away, we got on the field. On the opening offensive play, the coach called for me to get the ball. Like a person picking up a scalding hot object, I dropped it.

Instantly, I thought, *Dang, this is more of the same thing*. I came to the sidelines with my head down.

Coach Red hit me in the head and said, "Look, son, this is your game. Catch that ball and run."

The next play was for me, and not only did I catch the wet ball, but I ran it twelve more yards. The next play, Deuce ran it for ten hard yards. Then it was thrown to me on first and eight, and I caught it in the end zone. My first collegiate touchdown tasted sweeter than sugar. Wow, God was good! Not because He allowed me to be successful, but because He allowed me to be humble. He allowed me to learn that when I blocked out the rest of the world and focused on Him, I could do all things. He controlled everything. After getting that, I had the power—His power to be more than a conqueror and to be successful in riding out storms.

# ~ 3 ~

# Stacking the Deck

Boy, it sure felt great to win. I had finally gotten my form back, and after catching that first pass for a touchdown, it was on. Even being triple-teamed, I still managed to catch amazing balls. The Perry Skky Jr. that analysts predicted would do spectacular things in college had shown up.

It was a whole different feeling being on the victorious side of things. My teammates were smiling and giving me dap. Coach Red told me how outstanding I was. The press conference after the game went smoother than a wall sanded by a painter before being painted. I wasn't in the hot seat with anyone, and that felt pretty good.

Mario came up to me in the locker room and said, "Look, rookie, you gotta come to the after party."

"What, naw. That's not my thing, dude," I said to him. "I plan to hang out with my girl."

"Yeah, right. There'll be plenty of girls there. Forget about her."

Scratching my head, I said, "Naw, naw . . ."

Sticking his bad breath in my face, he said, "I guess you didn't hear what I said to you. You don't get a choice, freshman. You're going to show up at this party. You don't have to stay long, but you have to make an appearance. We clear?"

I huffed. When he didn't back down, I nodded. After he left, I hit my locker door.

"Hey, man, what's wrong with you?" Deuce said as he popped me in the back with a towel. "We did our thing tag-teaming them out there. If I wasn't running, you was catching that ball and making them Memphis Tigers want to be back at the zoo. You feelin' me?"

"Boy, you silly," I said. "They had me tamed for sure on that first play."

"I know, man. I guess we found our game with the cards we had. Put an ace after an ace on them. Oh, speaking of cards, let's play spades tonight," he said, thinking he had a novel idea.

"Can't, man. Mario wants me to do something."

"What, you his boy now?"

Popping him, I said, "Don't even start."

"I'm just saying, why do you feel obligated to go to his thing? You know they ain't going to be doing nothing but—"

"Yeah, I know!" I said, cutting him off and walking away before he could give me an explanation.

I had no idea what I was going to say to Savoy. I didn't want to leave her hanging. Since the two of us never came up with a place to meet, maybe I could just disappear for an hour or two. I didn't want to lie, but if I didn't see her in the crowd, how could she be mad at me, right? To my surprise, that plan went out the window when I found her standing right in between my parents, waiting on me with all of the other players' parents and friends. What was I going to do?

"Son, you did your thing," my dad said as he held out his hand for me to give him dap.

My mom just beamed with pride. Her wide smile made me feel proud. I gave her the biggest hug.

"Well, look who we found!" my mom said to me, motioning to Savoy as we came out of the embrace.

"Hey, Savoy." I slightly waved, but wasn't ready to stand by her side.

My dad chimed in. "Your sister called. Even though she's on the road, she heard you did good. Georgia still has to play Mississippi State today."

"Yeah, I'll call her later on." I placed my arm around my mom, inwardly not wanting them to go.

"Well, son, the crowd has died down. We're going to get on the road. We know you and Miss Lady here have some plans," my dad said to me.

Before I could stall them and have more time to figure out some kind of an excuse, my parents had vanished.

"Gosh, they jetted out of here, didn't they?" I said to Savoy.

"Your dad told me he was going to stop by his mom's house in Conyers," she said.

"Yeah, down in Covington."

"And then they were going to get back on to Augusta."

"That's a long drive."

"Yeah, that's true. So, where can we go to celebrate?" she asked. "I'm so proud of you."

"Uh, can we meet back up a little later?"

"Yeah, sure. Why?"

"Coach needs me to talk to some media and stuff," I said, knowing I was feeding her bull.

"Oh, yeah. Call my cell when you're done." She stroked my face with her soft hand.

"Sounds good." I felt so low and terrible for lying to her pretty behind.

In some kind of way, I was going to make it up to her. I certainly didn't want any lies between us, and though I considered this only a tiny white one, I was planning to make my time at Mario's jam quick.

Two hours later, I was still stuck at his party, which was

hosted by one of the local white fraternities. I couldn't believe Mario had it going on like that. I kept forgetting he was
mixed. He could roll with anyone. Not that I really cared. I
just needed him to give me the peace sign so I could be out.

Then I got tired of waiting on him, so I went up to him,
nestled in between two hotties, and said, "Look, it's a nice
thing you got here and everything, but I got stuff to do."

"Rookie, you need to wait up for a second. I need to rap
to you for a minute. Hold up, like you really got somewhere
to go."

He whispered in the ear of one of the girls, and she got
up, went over to a crew of about three other pretty little
girls, and brought them over to me. They pulled me onto the
dance floor and had me in the middle of some kind of trian-
gle rotating dance that I was starting to enjoy.

That was, until I heard Mario scream, "Saxon, you in the
house? Cool, boy."

Before I could look to see if he was alone, right behind
him was his sister, my girl, Savoy. She put her hands on her
hips. Her eyes were bloody. I knew she was ticked.

She stepped up to me and the girls. "I need to talk to you
right now."

I looked pitiful. I needed her to calm down. I didn't get
my wish.

"*You are such a liar!*" she screamed out.

She was correct, and I know it looked like more than what
it was, but I got completely offended that she was playing me
in front of all these people. She touched my arm, and I
jerked it back.

"Forget you then," she said before she rushed out of the
frat house.

Without even thinking, I dashed behind her and caught
her arm. "Wait, Savoy. I'm sorry."

"Get your hands off me," she said as I tried to stay close.

"What do you want to tell me, Perry? You want to tell me another lie? I'm sitting there waiting for you, and Saxon came
by and told me where you were. I don't know, I guess I
would have been sitting in the fool's chair all night."

"It's just a big misunderstanding. I know what it must
look like, but . . ."

"It looks like what it is. I even defended you against Sax.
Told him, 'No, he's with the coach somewhere,' and now
don't I just look like the biggest jerk in the world *believing
you*. I'm not enough for you, Perry, huh? You want to stack
up your playa cards with all of these women? Well, go ahead,
Perry. I won't stand in your way."

She turned to walk away.

"No, wait, wait!" I said, moving my body in front of hers.
"Truth is, our quarterback told me I had to come."

"My brother said he was given that same order, but if you
would have told me that was the case, I would have never—"

"I know, I know, but I just didn't know how it would ap-
pear telling you I had to go to some party. That just sounded
like a lie, too."

"So, instead of giving me the benefit of the doubt that I
would believe the truth, you just made up something. I have
a brother who plays the game of football. A wild brother,
might I add. I would have said okay, you have to go. I understand it's all a part of hazing. I get that thing. What I don't get
is you enjoying it. Seeing you on that dance floor with those
girls' hands touching you all over your body—I just can't be
a part of that. I just don't think the cards are in favor of us,
you know?"

And then she left me there.

Sunday morning, I was awakened by the voice of my
grandmother on my answering machine, "Perry, Perry, this your
grandma. Pick up, boy. I know you ain't at nobody's church."

"Hey, Grandma," I groggily responded.

"I know you a big football player now, boy. All my neighbors can't believe you're my grandson. But shoot, I remember when you were in diapers."

"Yes ma'am. You right, Grandma."

She asked, "You don't have the big head now, do you?"

"No, ma'am. How you doing?" I said, now remembering that she had cancer. She was using unconventional methods of medicine to deal with the pain.

"I'm still smoking a little here and there, and not just cigarettes. You know what I mean, baby?"

"Come on, Grandma."

"I still wouldn't wish this illness on my worst enemy, and I do have a worst enemy—lady down the street tried to seduce your grandfather back in the day. I ain't forgot, but I wouldn't even want her to have cancer. This thing can weigh you down."

"I'm sorry, Grandma." I knew I needed to pray for her more.

"Everybody has their cross to bear. Don't be sad for me. I'ma be alright."

She just tripped me out. She was so much fun, so honest, and so real.

"Hey, I'm fixin' a big ol' dinner. I want you to bring a few of your friends down here and eat."

"Oh, Grandma, I don't know if we can. We have meetings with the coach and stuff."

"Well, next Sunday, who do I need to call to get you excused from all of that? A boy needs to spend some time with his grandmother. I'm sick and everything, too. I could be dead tomorrow."

*"Grandma!"*

"What, boy, the truth is the light. You gonna die, too, you know? I want you to come visit me."

"Well, we do get a small break," I said, thinking about her collards. "But it won't be 'til late tonight."

"Well, I don't want you on the road late and stuff. I do want you to call me and make sure my heart is still ticking. I'm expecting you to be here next Sunday now."

"Yes, ma'am, I will be."

"I know your granddaddy up there now, smiling down. He loved all of that ol' football stuff. Your daddy and your uncle were just wimps. After somebody hit them, they screamed, 'I don't want to play anymore,' but you, Junior, you're tough. Your grandfather would be real proud. I guess they have them digital TVs in heaven. I could see him sitting back wishing he had some of my sweet tea, bragging to all of the disciples that you was his boy."

I laughed. "Grandma, you so funny!"

At that moment, it was clear to me that I needed to talk to her more often. Not only was she a hoot, but she had such a fun view of life. My stress was lifted spending time with her.

"Naw, baby, I'm just old. I couldn't imagine what heaven is really like. I bet it's even better than I'm describing to you."

"Don't talk like that, Grandma."

"Boy, please, I just told you we all got to go. Ain't nothing wrong with getting excited about it."

Looking at my ceiling, I said, "I guess you're right."

Later that night, I was at the table playing spades with my roommates. Though Collin wasn't as happy-go-lucky as Deuce, Lance, and me, he was becoming more normal and no longer staying so cooped-up in his room all day. It was good downtime for us.

Lance looked at Deuce and me, and said, "Man, y'all are so lucky."

Deuce dealt the cards and said, "Don't start now. Let's all enjoy our time. So we're in the starting lineup. Your time is coming."

"When?" Lance said.

"And for real, there is a whole lot of pressure out there," I added as I collected my hand.

"I'm up for the challenge," he said, frowning at his cards. "If you can do it, I can do it."

"Yeah, I know!" I said, trying to keep the peace with him.

"You guys think it's nothing for us to want to get out there and show our stuff," Collin said in a very serious tone. "You don't know what it's like to be on the sidelines, as clean at the end of the game as when you came in. No grass stains or dirt anywhere."

"Boy, you a kicker. How you ever gonna get grass stains?" Deuce asked.

I hit Deuce in his arm and said to Collin, "I hear you. I understand. But it's not that cool when you get a chance and you screw it up. People still talking about the game I lost last week."

"Whatever," Lance said. "It's not all your fault. I've been watching Mario's passes. Some of his stuff is real iffy."

"Boy, you just saying that because you want to play."

"You don't have to believe me. I'm with him all day. I know what he does and what he is capable of. I know the crazy, messed-up passes he throws from time to time that just don't make sense. I don't know. There's something fishy going on about that."

Then there was a knock at our door.

"Go away, Sax, we don't have no food," Lance yelled out.

"It's Savoy," a female voice replied. "Is Perry there?"

Quickly, I got up from the table. She hadn't called me all day, and I still felt bad about her leaving me the way she did after she caught me in my fib.

Lance yelled, "Dang, man. Now you gonna stop the game for a girl."

"Lance, hush." I looked over and put my finger on my lips.

"For real, you know Perry gets all crappy when 'love' ain't worked out," Deuce teased.

"Can I talk to you, please?" she said when I opened the door.

She waved at my roommates and walked in to my room. "I have had time to think about it, and it just seems to me that no matter how hard I try, I want a little bit more from our relationship than you do."

"No, don't say that," I said to her.

"It's true." She stared me down and dared me to deny it.

I hated to admit it, but she was right. I felt a little smothered. She was the only girl I wanted to be with at the moment, but I didn't want to be with her 24-7, and it seemed that if it were up to her, that would be the case. I believe that if she could, she'd be lining up with me at football practice just to make sure we were around each other.

I grabbed her hands and said, "I don't want to break up or nothing. Can't you just back off some? I know it seems crazy for me to say, but trust me."

"Yeah, it's crazy for me to trust a dude who lies to my face."

"I didn't feel like I could be honest. I felt like you would think I was a punk not able to stand up to some of the players on my team. I'm just trying to find my way, Savoy. I'm not always going to make the right decision. I mess up sometimes, and I just don't know how much right I can do for you, you know?"

Then she started to cry.

"What's wrong? What's going on?"

"It's been a couple of weeks since we've been together, and my cycle hasn't come on."

"What you trying to say to me? You've taken a pregnancy test or something?"

"No, but what if we're pregnant?"

I just held her in my arms and told her it was going to be okay. Of course, I didn't know if that was the truth, but I think it was something that the both of us sure needed to hear. To win anything, I knew I needed God in the midst of it, so I prayed: "Lord, Savoy and I made a mistake, and we're asking right now, Father, if You could not make it another mistake. If it turns out that she is pregnant, I know that You will turn it into good. We love You, and we thank You for letting us come to You even in our brokenness. We trust that You will keep this situation whole and help us learn how to be in the right relationship with You and with each other. In Jesus's name, we pray. Amen."

She squeezed me tight. Maybe we would be okay after all.

It felt good keeping my head on straight. It made the week zoom by faster than a race car doing a lap. If I wasn't in class, I was studying for a class. If I wasn't on the practice field, I was in my room going over plays. If I wasn't thinking about Savoy, I was talking to her, trying to keep her calm.

Waiting for the results to flow in our favor kept me on edge. However, staying prayerful helped me not to worry. Talking to God gave me the strength I needed to not be stressed, to not be overconfident, to just keep the status quo. Staying connected to the Big Man made me feel good.

So in the second home game and third regular-season battle, I was ready to run up to score. I was ready to catch all kinds of passes, to make this an offensive display. After all, we were scheduled to play Stanford, just a Pac-10 school, but definitely respectable. I certainly didn't want to take it for granted.

I was really psyched when Mario came up to me after I was dressed in my pads, ready for warm-ups, and said, "Look, we need to keep some excitement."

"Yeah, let's try to get a hundred today. This is basketball, baby," I said, jumping.

"Naw, naw, man. That's not what I'm saying. We need to keep it close."

"What you talking about?" I squinted my eyes like he was speaking Chinese.

He leaned in toward me. "You know, let's win, but keep it close. You know, so the fans feel like they are getting a good game. Feel me?"

"Man, that's crazy." I turned away to get ready to jog to the field. "Just throw me the ball."

"Man, you don't hear me," he mumbled as I put distance between us.

Lance came up to me, and we both walked out. "What did he ask you?"

"I don't know. He was talking stupid." I could not make sense of Mario's warped strategy.

Lance jerked my jersey. "Something is going on with him."

"Lance, come on, man. Just be ready when it's your chance. Don't hate. He's a senior."

"Something ain't right, Perry. I can't explain it. Something is messed up with him."

I just passed it off as Lance being overly excited to get his chance to shine. So I jogged away from his tail as well. At that point, I felt both he and Mario had issues. However, I was determined not to let either of them ruin my game.

When our offense stepped out on the field for the first play from scrimmage, the offensive line held tight and gave protection. However, Mario went outside the pocket and got tackled. Then it happened again. I scratched my head, which was hard to do because I had on a helmet. I was dumbfounded by his stupid moves. When we finally got the ball back after defense stopped the Cardinal on three and out, I was wide open. Mario overthrew me on two plays. Thankfully Coach called for Deuce to get the ball, and he ran it in for a touchdown.

The rest of the game continued that way. Though we pulled a win, by the end it was too close for comfort, and even some of our fans booed. I wasn't interviewed, but I certainly crossed my hands and watched the media scold Mario, calling him inconsistent, a loose cannon, and nastier things of that magnitude. It sort of made me think, *Dang, was Lance right?* Was something else going on with Mario that was making him be so sporadic on purpose?

The next day, I appeased my grandmother, thanks to Coach giving us a little extra time off. I went over to her house to eat some chitlings, ham, collard greens, mashed potatoes, macaroni and cheese, and lumpy cornbread.

"Grandma, you got so much food here, I can't eat all of this." I felt honored, but I didn't bring teammates.

"Child, all of this ain't for you. I'ma have a few more mouths to feed a little later on. I just hope they all don't come at the same time, you know?"

I asked, "What you talking about?" I was pretty sure she wasn't talking about another male.

"I got new floors in my house, boy. Didn't you notice? You know I didn't pay for them, but somebody had to do them." She smiled wider than a mile. "Mr. James did 'em, and then Mr. Saunders—you know, the man down the street cuts my grass every week, edges, and all of that stuff. I can't give them no lovin'—too old for that—but I sure can feed their bellies. Ain't nothing wrong with having a few friends. You a popular little football player. You got all them females around you, you know what I'm saying?"

"Grandma."

"Mmm, I ain't dead."

"Grandma, you need to slow down. Do I need to come

down here more often and check out these males you talking about?"

"Whatever, boy, you need to do something with your head. Are you growing a 'fro? Spending so much time with that football, you ain't got time to take care of yourself? I told your momma Georgia Tech was going to be a hard school. You should have went to my alma mater, Fort Valley State."

"Yeah, Grandma, you're right," I said, not wanting to have a debate with her.

"Don't be quick to hush me up. That's a good school."

"Grandma, I know. My boy Damarius is there, remember?" She nodded her head. "I just had a scholarship and all."

"Yeah, well, go do something with your hair. That mall barbershop—they're open every day."

"How you know that, Grandma?"

" 'Cause Mr. James's son owns it, and he ain't nothing but trouble. Watch yourself over there. If you tell 'em I sent you, you'll be fine."

"Grandma, you don't know drug dealers, do you?"

"I can handle myself, child. Plus, where you think I get my loot from? His granddaddy won't believe me. He think just because he got a barbershop, he's legit. Who got a barbershop that open on a Sunday? That's the Lord's day. Everything is supposed to be closed, unless you a heathen." She touched my growing and mangled afro. "But I sure am happy he is open today because you need something done to that there head."

"Yes, ma'am."

I gave her a kiss, packed me up a big plate for later that evening, and headed out. I thought going to the mall for a cut wouldn't be a bad idea because I could also pick up a little card and chain for Savoy. Walking to the hair spot, I was stopped dead in my tracks when I saw Mario talking to some man inside the shop.

I backed up and peeked in. Something made me eavesdrop. As intense as their conversation seemed, I felt uneasy about his involvement.

I could hear Mario say, "It was hard to keep the score like that, man." Then I saw him collect some money. I couldn't even walk in there. My head was gonna have to stay jacked-up. I turned around and walked away. What had I walked up on? What was Mario doing to our team? Was he drowning our games on purpose, trying to keep the scores tight? Even a fool could put those pieces together. What was I going to do, now that I knew he was betting and stacking the deck?

# ~ 4 ~

# Catching Something Awful

"Okay, why are we going on a triple date again?" I said to Savoy as we walked around the upscale and bumping outdoor mall, Atlantic Station.

"Please, don't give me drama," she said in a way that let me know I was still in the doghouse for lying a few days back.

Trying to say the right thing, I replied, "I just wanted to spend some time with you."

"Well, where's my brother?"

"That boy don't have no problem getting a girl," I said, letting her know I thought this idea was loony.

"I know, but he always meets the wrong kind of girl. And then there's your roommate. You speak so highly of Deuce. You're always saying he still has a broken heart over his high school sweetheart. I've met some cool girls. I'm trying to establish some relationships apart from you."

"I know."

"Plus, when females find out I know football players—fine football players at that—I have to try hooking them up, come on. Honestly, I'm just trying to figure some folks out."

I put my hand behind her head and rubbed her neck. "I want you to have some good friends."

"These are some of the girls from the track team I have

been working with, and you're a good judge of character. So I know you'll tell me if you think they're cool or not."

I nodded, remembering how foul her high school friend who proved not to be a friend at all was. That chick came on to me in front of Savoy and my mom. I didn't want this to happen again.

We all were supposed to meet at the ice cream parlor in the complex. My boy Deuce and Savoy's brother Saxon were running late. I knew it was probably Saxon's fault, primpin' in the mirror. As the two girls walked toward us, I hoped they'd get here soon.

"Hey, y'all." Savoy lit up, dashed over to the two girls, hugged them, and then motioned me over there. "Come here, baby." She held out her hand, and I grabbed it. "This is Jailyn." Jailyn reminded me of my cousin Pillar, who was really light-skinned. I couldn't tell if Jailyn was mixed or black. She was about five four, light, had blue-green eyes that spoke sincerity, and seemed kind of bashful.

"It's nice to meet you," Jailyn said, hardly looking at me. "We see you all over the TV screen, it seems like I already know you. Keep up the good work."

"Thanks," I said, a little reserved.

Then there was this barracuda-looking girl with what I assumed was a weave spiraling down her back. Though I wasn't a hairdresser, I did know there should not be a place where you could see where the hair ended and the weave began. Her clothes were really tight. Yeah, it was still hot, but it wasn't summertime.

"And this is Charlie. Ooh, Jailyn, I've got to tell you something," Savoy abruptly said as she pulled her girl to the side and left me all alone with the girl whose mouth looked like it wanted to bite me.

Trying to get her to remember lines you don't cross, I said, "So, Savoy tells me you guys are real good friends?"

"Huh? No, we're just teammates. She just thinks I can tame her brother." Interesting choice of words, I thought, but I was certainly glad because I wanted Deuce to be introduced to the sweeter girl of the two. This Charlie girl was certainly not it.

Then she slid over to me like a little snake and said, "If I don't find her brother hot, then . . ." she started to bat her eyes.

Before she could even finish, Savoy came back with Jailyn. "What are y'all talking about?"

She could see in my face that all wasn't normal. It felt too rude for me to say, "You need to watch out for this one." I didn't want Savoy to think I sent off the wrong signals to Charlie. Plus, maybe I was overthinking it. Some women's personalities were flirty. Although, she had made it clear she had no loyalty to Savoy. Yeah, this evening was going to prove very interesting.

As I listened to them jibber-jabber for about five minutes, I said, "Can I get y'all some ice cream?"

I was trying to wait on the fellas, but I didn't want the line to get too long. After I took their orders, it was my pleasure to give them space. I looked back out the window and saw Savoy so happy to be talking to the two of them. She wanted friends badly. Would one of the two be enough for her?

When I got back outside, Charlie said, "Hey, I think we have a class together."

Trying desperately not to have any connection with her, I said, "No, I don't think we do."

"Yeah, I think we have calculus together." There were 200-plus students in that room. Though I always looked for the sisters, I truly hadn't seen her. Now that I knew she was sneaky, I didn't want to see her again.

Finally, the guys walked up. Charlie didn't even wait for Savoy to introduce her. She sashayed her way over to Saxon.

"I'm Charlie London. Your sister has shown me tons of your photos. You look even cuter in person." Saxon grinned, unaware of the game that was being played on him. "Let's go walking and get to know each other." I shook my head when I saw Charlie take his hand and squeeze his butt.

"Dang, girl, you're a little fresh, ain't you?" Saxon said, as he put his hand on her shoulder and they walked away. "See y'all."

Jailyn was blushing as she glanced at my boy. The way Deuce was checking her out, I knew he was very interested. Maybe one connection would work out.

"Jailyn Richards," Savoy said, "this is Perry's roommate, Deuce Avery. Deuce, this is my new friend Jailyn.

They shook hands. Jailyn got a little bit of the ice cream on Deuce's shirt. She started freaking out, searching for napkins and frowning and all.

"I'm so sorry," Jailyn said, sticking her finger out to catch the ice cream before it made a bigger mess.

"No, that's okay," Deuce said calmly. "I'm a football player, not a pretty boy."

"Here's a napkin," Savoy said, trying to hand it to Deuce.

Jailyn took it. She dabbed the shirt off herself. The two of them started walking in front of Savoy and me.

Atlantic Station was a nice hangout spot. I went there a few times during the summer. All kinds of shops, people here and there, restaurants—just an all-around cool atmosphere.

Savoy said, "So what do you think? Did I make good matches? Good friends? Your thoughts? Tell me. Tell me."

"Girl, it's too early to tell. We've been here for only forty minutes or so."

Females kill me with how they like to rush everything. Granted, a dude may want to get in bed when he first sees a chick, but all them feelings and stuff were a little too much. I had to calm her down.

She called her brother on the cell phone and told him to meet us at the pizza joint. As I was walking through the door, I felt something touch my back pocket. I turned around and noticed it was Charlie's hand. When I got to the table, I reached in the pocket myself and saw that she had put her number in there. Underneath the number, wrote, "Call me so I can give you a good time." I felt sick for real.

I told Savoy, "Hey, um, I'm not feeling good. Can we just skip out? Take a few slices to go?"

"You're not going yet, are you, Perry?" Charlie winked when only I was looking at her face. "We're just now getting to know each other."

"Yeah, man. Don't be a wimp. Drink some water or something," Saxon called out.

I ignored them. I politely told Deuce and Jailyn that I would see them later. Savoy and I got takeout, and we were out. In the car, I could tell Savoy was a little mad at me. Her little lips were pouting and stuff. It was actually sort of cute. But you know, I didn't know what to do. She seemed so into both of those girls. Was it wrong for me to jump in and break her heart when it wasn't about anything. I wasn't sure how to address it, so for now, she was just going to have to be mad. She had a good guy who got her away from some phoniness, right?

I guess you should speak only the positive because sometimes, you can bring unwanted things upon yourself. The night before, the only way I was able to get away from Charlie was by telling Savoy I was sick. Now, as I woke up to go to class, my head felt as though a ton of bricks was on it. I couldn't even lift up. No covers were on me, and the sheets were soaked like I had gotten out of the shower and not wiped off. My body was aching more than if I had six defensive players on top of me. My throat felt a little scratchy, and I let out a little squeal.

"Dang it," I shouted. "I think I have the flu."

None of my three roommates had the same class schedule as me. If I skipped calculus, my first class of the day, maybe I would have enough energy to make it to the other two. Then I could go see the trainer. He could pump me up with a little something to make me feel better, and that should be it. So I dialed up the emergency phone number, and one of our assistant trainers picked up the phone,

In a weak tone I said, "Man, I don't feel good."

"You don't sound good, Perry."

"I'm thinking I could come by and you could check me out. I'm pretty sure it's the flu, though."

"We got a big game, though—first ACC and Coastal Division rival. You probably need to stay in bed all day. We'll make sure the academic advisors get what you need. Deuce is in the whirlpool now."

"What's up with him?"

"You know your roommate is tough. Just a couple of nicks he's trying to straighten out. I'll send some cold medicine his way. Take it as prescribed, and you'll feel a little better tomorrow."

"Alright, thanks, man."

An hour later, Deuce had to bang on my door to get me to open it. I needed to take my medicine. It was nighttime before I woke up again.

My phone rang, and it was Savoy. "Hey, babe."

In a panicked tone, she said, "What's wrong? My brother said somebody said you were with the trainer?"

Upset, I said, "He's got to quit."

"What do you mean? You know he told me because he knew I'd be concerned."

"Yeah, but I don't want you to be concerned. Seems like you know stuff before I do, and it's my own life."

"You're being facetious."

"No, Savoy, I'm just being real. I don't like that."

"Well, I'm worried about you. I'm on my way over to bring you some chicken soup."

"My roommates took care of all of that, and the trainers fixed me up. I'm good. I just need to rest right now." I was so weak.

"You're not worried about me and the baby or anything like that, are you?"

Easing her mind, I said, "Savoy, I think I got the flu, girl. I don't know how, but I just need to rest up. I gotta be ready for this game this weekend. You don't need to stress out over something until we know what we are dealing with, right?"

"Yeah," she said in a tone more deflated than a tire with no air. "You sure you don't need me to come over? Alright. Well, I'll call you back before the night is over."

"If I'm not dead to the world, then it's cool. I'll be alright. I know you'll pray for me."

No sooner had I hung up the phone than my head hit the pillow. I always appreciated that even if my door was unlocked, Deuce would knock on it. Lance, on the other hand, never was that courteous. He simply tried the handle, and if it worked, he was in.

Lance annoyingly flicked my lights on and off. "Boy, wake up, wake up!"

"What? What?" I said in a groggy tone.

"You ain't telling me you was tipping out on Savoy."

"I'm not, man. What are you talking about?"

"Man, you got a nice honey in the crib."

I said, "Why you always sound so black?"

"What?" Lance said as he pushed me back onto the bed.

"Stop, man. I'm weak."

I heard a familiar female voice. "That's okay, Lance. He doesn't have to get up. I thought I'd bring his homework. I'll make him feel a little better and be out of here."

I had to wipe my eyes. What in the world was Charlie doing here? I found some energy from somewhere and jumped up.

Shocked, I said, "Come on, what you doing? This is my room. What you doing?" She escorted my roommate out and closed the door behind him.

She tried to touch my chest before I reached for a shirt. "I just wanted to talk to you. You weren't in calculus today. Savoy said she was worried about you. Something about a cold. So I figured I'd come by with some Halls."

"Hey, my girl thinks y'all are cool. Though I appreciate you bringing the homework, you got to go." She leaned in and tried to wipe my brow. I grabbed her hand and said, "Listen very clearly. Ain't nothing happening with us, okay?"

"Okay, whatever." She stomped off.

I knew she wasn't happy, but I was more pissed off that she'd come to my room thinking that I thought she was fine and would get with her.

Lance opened my door again and said, "Well, you should have at least introduced her to me if you were going to be finished with her that quickly."

"Get out," I said, grabbing my stomach, still aching all over.

"You ain't feeling no better? Get rested up because we do need you Saturday."

"Oh, so you don't want Mario to do bad?"

"He'll hang himself."

I was too tired to talk to Lance about me having my eye on

him, too, so I just let it ride. Deep down I agreed with him, though.

The phone rang, and I picked it up, as I recognized the number on the caller ID. "Hey, Savoy."

"I just wanted to tell you good-night, baby."

"I'm alright. Now get your rest."

I hate that you've been over there all day by yourself. I'm coming over tomorrow."

"I'm going to be better tomorrow, girl." And then I started coughing. I don't know if I was coughing because I was physically choked up or because I was making myself sick over hiding something. I hadn't been here alone. Either way, I had to hang up the phone so she wouldn't be able to see through what I wasn't saying.

Thankfully, on Saturday, I was ready to go. We were in Raleigh, North Carolina, about to take on the Blue Devils. It was fun being in the city that had heavily recruited me. I liked that my confidence was coming back. My focus was in place. I wanted to make a dent in the game of football. My grandmother just told me how much my grandfather loved the game. How did I know he wasn't up there orchestrating my steps with God? I knew he had big shoes. I was getting ready to fill them.

Coach came over and said, "Alright, Perry, I don't have time for coughing and sneezing. If you need to be benched because you're too weak to play, let me know now. I don't want you to get out there and let us down."

"No, Coach, I'm ready." When he left me, I bumped into Mario on his cell phone.

"Watch it, dude," Mario said.

I couldn't even excuse myself because if he had been looking up instead of crunching numbers, he wouldn't have run into me. I was tired of playing punk to these upper classmen. My football career was very important to me. I had the pros in sight, even though they were still a ways away. I wanted to take one game at a time. I wasn't going to let Mario or a dollar here or there get in the way. If he was doing something shady, I was going to call his butt out on it.

"Hold on, Jack," he said into the receiver. "Perry, move out of my way."

"I see you got an attitude. There's no need to take it out on me."

He got louder. "I said, get out of my way."

"You can walk around," I told him bluntly.

He was shorter than me and not as built. He had a bark, but I had a bite. He was conducting some kind of business he didn't want me to hear. He gave in and walked around me.

"Yeah, that's what I thought," I said.

Fifteen minutes before the game, Coach called us in for our last locker-room talk. "Just so you guys understand, this is ACC play. It's time to shine if we want to look good at the end of the season. We're already playing catch-up. Our competitors in the conference are already ahead of us because of our first loss. However, let's start getting neck to neck with these teams."

Coach Red had a way of speaking that captured our attention. He was a motivator. I loved his zeal for the game. It was contagious. You could not hear a sound.

He continued, "We can win this thing. Now don't be fooled. This is a good Blue Devils team. However, I'm here today to tell you that they are not better than the Yellow Jackets."

We all started screaming, ready to get out on the field and start rumbling. When we were up 21 to 0, I thought maybe I misjudged Mario. Then the next two offensive drives he threw invited direct interceptions. We're on one side of the field and he throws the ball to the other. It just didn't make any sense. Something shady was going on. Now it was 21 to

14. I started to go over to him while Coach Red was chomping his butt out and say, "Bench him, bench him, bench him."

I watched his eyes, and I ran in that direction. I was able to make something out of nothing.

Later, Lance came to my end and said, "I told you that boy ain't right. Why won't Coach let me in? Either somebody has something on him or . . . or . . . I just can't figure it out, Perry. It's not right, and I deserve to be in there. Especially if he's going to screw up like that. Coach gives him tons of chances and . . ."

"Alright, alright, it's game time, man."

All I could do was pray: *Lord, all I do in this game is lift You up. I'm just trying to make You proud of what I do. I'm not trying to falsely accuse somebody of cheating or doing something wrong. I simply want to win it for the team. Can you help me do that?* I didn't want to get Mario's bad attitude, and praying sort of calmed me.

The chaplain came over to me and said, "I saw you talking to the Lord. Keep executing both ways. You're going to come up big for us."

"Coach just needs to give me the ball, and I can run the clock out and we can win," Deuce said to me on the sidelines.

When we got into the huddle and learned the play was a pass, a yucky sensation ran up my spine. My number was up, and I didn't have any confidence in Mario. Thankfully, I wasn't blinded by the light, because even though he was throwing a Hail Mary toward the end zone, I could find the speed to make the play. I had been so weak a few days earlier that I really had to find the strength to hightail it into fast gear. I zoomed when I started to think about why I was really here.

I thought about my granddad and ran. I thought about my parents and ran a little faster. I thought about Savoy, and I thought about my sister, and I went a little faster. I thought about the team and the ball that was trying to get away from me, and the crowd was dead silent, but the Tech fans that traveled with us were screaming.

"Dang, man, you a bad man," Deuce said to me.

"You so silly."

"For real, for real. You got mad skills."

"That's what I'm talking about," Lance said. I was getting lots of accolades from the sidelines.

"Seems like that cold is gone, son," Coach Red said. "Twenty-seven to fourteen. I think you won it for us. Though that pass was a tough one, you looked good catching something awful."

# ~ 5 ~

# Laying Down Facts

"**B**oy, doesn't it feel good to be home?" Deuce said as we entered our apartment after a victorious game over the Blue Devils.

We had two away games, and I could tell being away was not going to be fun. Don't get me wrong, we stayed at nice hotels. We ate good food. We had police escorts. Even though my newfound quarters weren't the home I grew up in, they certainly were comfortable, and all four of us were glad to be back.

"Florida State's playing Boston College tonight," Lance said, grabbing the remote.

"That's good. One of them will end up with a loss and be equal with us," I said, trying to calculate what it would take for us to become conference champs.

"I'm a little tired. You all can watch it," Collin said.

"Please, don't be a party pooper," Lance called after him.

None of us knew what was going on with Collin. However, the word on the team was that his kicking game was becoming worse. I wanted to say something to keep his moral up, but I knew how it felt when your game wasn't on. It was something he would have to work out on his own.

"See, that's what I'm talking about. If it would've been my

old coach, he would have benched a poor performer and put somebody else in. He gave this guy fifty thousand chances," Lance screamed out.

I put the popcorn in the microwave and walked over to the TV. Seeing the replay of our quarterback throwing countless bad passes just made me scratch my head. This wasn't right.

"Yeah, he did look sort of awful. Aw, Perry, look at your catch man," Deuce said as I stepped away from the TV to get the popcorn, which was done.

"I saw, man."

"Look at that bad catch. I still don't know how you made that one. Boy, you're tough," Deuce said, holding out his hand for me to slap.

"Thanks," I said as I gave him five.

I really appreciated living in an atmosphere that was mostly positive. I had some work to do with Collin. Lance was so into his own position. He was not a fan of mine, but I was grateful he was not a foe either. Deuce was in my corner all the way. He was equally talented.

"Uh-oh, check it out. You're up for one of the national plays of the week. Go, boy!" Deuce said to me.

"Thank goodness you were able to catch something," Lance said. "If you wouldn't have, there's no telling what would have happened to us."

Contemplating talking to them about all I suspected was weighing me down. I was fed up with Mario's playing. I knew he was jilting the team. Normally, it wasn't for me to get in other people's business, but I needed somebody to help me figure this whole thing out.

"Can I talk to y'all?" Still a little unsure of what I was going to say.

"Dang, this sounds serious," Deuce said, sliding over so I could share the long couch.

"Hey, Collin, come here," I yelled out as I sat down.

"Yeah?" he said, peeping around the corner.

I said, "I know you're tired, man, but I wanted to talk to everybody for a minute."

"Everything okay, Perry?" he asked in a concerned voice from his door.

"I don't know." I bit my tongue, hoping this discussion was the right move.

Lance grabbed the bowl of popcorn off the table and placed it in his lap. He and Deuce started munching away. Collin came in, but looked like I needed to hurry up and get to it.

"I think Mario is betting on our games." Lance got up so fast that the popcorn spilled all over the couch and the floor.

"Boy, dang!" Deuce yelled at his clumsiness.

Lance paced back and forth. "Naw, naw, this is crazy, see. That's what I have been saying. Everything wasn't right with him. Nobody wanted to believe me. Now. Now . . . *now*? Finally, after he's almost thrown away the easiest game in the world, somebody listens." Lance came over and shook my hand. "Thank you."

"Boy, stop," I said, taking my hand away.

"No, I'm serious, Perry. Why you think he is? And I tell you why I think he is," Lance said as he bent down to start picking up popcorn.

"A couple of times, he hemmed me up and told me I needed to make sure that I did not mess up his flow. He had a lot invested in the game. Words like that. I didn't really give it too much thought then."

"I don't know," Deuce said to us. "Those are some big accusations. And I can't . . . I can't believe that."

"Well, I wish that was all," I said, sliding to the edge of the couch.

I had to lean over and show them that I had seriousness in

my eyes. "I knew this was a lot to say about somebody. Mario is cool. Heck, he is the leader of our team. No way in the world would I accuse him of something if I knew he wasn't doing something severely wrong. If I didn't believe this in the core of my being, I wouldn't bring it up."

Deuce said, "But, what else? I mean, what else do you have, Perry? Dang, if this got out, who knows what would happen to our team. The media is already cruel enough."

Bluntly I said, "I saw him getting paid off for a win."

"When? Where did you see this?" Deuce asked me, extremely upset.

"It was in a barbershop out y'all's way," I explained, pointing to him and Lance.

"Case closed then," Lance said, as if what I'd said was law.

"What do you know about what goes on in a black barbershop?" Deuce said to Lance.

"Everybody knows what goes on in the barbershop at *that* mall," Lance said, defending himself.

"I just didn't know college sports could be this brutal," Collin said. "I feel so much pressure to make every kick in practice, and practice is the place where you are supposed to be able to make mistakes. And now you're telling me our quarterback is probably throwing games."

"I just don't believe it." Deuce threw up his hands and began to pace.

"I wouldn't lie and make that up," I said defiantly to all three of them.

Lance put all of the popcorn in the trash. Quickly, he put on his tennis shoes. He then grabbed his jacket. "Well, come on, let's go."

"What do you mean?" Collin said, surely reading my mind.

"Yeah, what do you mean?" Deuce echoed, as if he thought Lance was cuckoo.

"I'm staying out of this," Collin said.

"We don't even know if Perry saw what he saw. He just saw something. Probably didn't even confront Mario. Did you talk to him yet?" Deuce asked me.

"Naw, I didn't. I wanted to run it by you guys. See what you thought."

"Well, I think we need to go to Coach Red right now," Lance said boldly. "Get him kicked off the team before the NCAA finds out and messes up our season."

"You just exaggerating the seriousness of this. All you want is to get your tail on the field." Deuce was now up in Lance's face.

"Okay, it is my information to tell," I said, stepping between them. "Both of you need to calm down. Forget I even mentioned it."

"What do you mean, forget it?" Lance said.

"Nobody can forget you said it," Deuce replied. "I just don't know if I believe it."

"Well, I believe it wholeheartedly," Lance said.

I still didn't know what I needed to do with the information about Mario. Now I saw that telling them was a bad mistake. Deuce was mad at me for selling out a brother. Collin was even more scared than he had been. Lance was ready to start a revolt.

Thank goodness Florida State made a long touchdown. That play drew all of us to the tube. On the next drive, BC did the same. The game went to commercial with a score of 7 to 7.

I said to them, "Look, guys, let me just think about this, okay?"

Deuce and Collin nodded. After I stared Lance down, he agreed. It was now an even bigger mess. Hopefully I could contain it. But how?

\* \* \*

"What's so urgent?" I said, a little irritated, when I drove up to Savoy's dorm directly after practice.

She said she needed to see me ASAP. Quite frankly, the tone of her voice when she called my cell, after I had a full day, really annoyed me. I wasn't going to come, but I knew she would blow up my cell if I didn't. I knew I would also regret coming to see her, so I figured I might as well get the talk over.

She got in my car and closed the door, and we drove off. "We need to talk."

"Okay, what's up?"

"You lied to me, Perry."

"What are you talking about?" She treated me like her pet, like she needed to know exactly where I was at all times.

"Girl, you have my class schedule. My momma don't even have that. You know where I am twenty-four–seven. What are you talking about?"

"Last week, when you told me you were all sick. Remember, you didn't want any visitors." She wasn't backing down on her claim.

All of a sudden, I had a clue to where this was going. Somehow she found out her friend Charlie came to visit me. I'd even forgotten why I didn't tell her. Of course, now that she was ready to blast me, I wished I had come clean.

I looked away, and Savoy said, "Oh, so you know what I'm talking about?"

"Look, I couldn't stop the girl from coming to see me," I blurted out, unable to protect Savoy's feelings.

If she wanted to be all big and bad and accuse me, she needed to understand the real deal. Her so-called friend was anything but. Yeah, that was why I didn't say anything.

"It's not about you stopping her. I have my own issues with Charlie. She's made it real clear that she wants you."

"Huh, why didn't you tell me?"

"I never thought you'd let her get close to you," Savoy said. "She told me how she came into your room and petted you and rubbed your back."

"What? That's a lie!"

"So she didn't pet you or come into your room?"

"No, no, she came into my room. But all this petting and touching and all of that stuff, no. You should know none of that happened. I don't think I have to defend myself to you. I care about you, Savoy. But you are all on my back like you don't trust me and stuff."

"How can I trust you? Everywhere I go, some girl some-where is talking about how fine you are."

"So, what does that mean?"

"It shouldn't matter, but it does."

"I tried to tell you how committed I am to you," I said.

I pulled the car up to the side of Campus Road. I had to look her in the eye. She had to see I cared about her. She didn't need to be worried about anybody else. Yeah, I wasn't com-pletely open and honest, but dang, I wasn't two-timing her either.

"You know, I don't even know why I care," she said, her eyes welling up with tears.

"What do you mean, you don't know why?"

"My brother told me everything about when she came over with practically no clothes on. And I confronted her. The little wench told me how y'all almost slept together."

"Oh, so Saxon is still up in my business. Anything he says is gold? Why you got to question her about it? Why didn't you come to me first off?"

"Well, I had come to you. That night, I asked if you were alone all day. I felt bad and wanted to pet you myself. You practically ordered me to stay away. Now I find out the rea-son you did not want me around was that she was probably in the room the entire time. Were you two laughing behind my back? If you want to be with her, Perry, then just go for it."

I pulled her completely close to me and just kissed her. My lips felt the groove for about thirty seconds or so. She needed to know that she and I had chemistry.

"Now, can't you see why I don't want her? I want you."

"I'm sorry," Savoy said as she pulled back a little. "I just can't do this."

"Why?"

"We're just not in the same place. You're a superstar up here."

"It's not like you're a regular student either. You may make the Olympics." She wasn't moved, so I addressed another issue that connected us. "Besides, you might be pregnant."

"Aw, well, if that's the only reason you're staying with me, you're off the hook. I'm not."

"Hey, why are you talking so harshly?" I tried to keep her in my arms, but she pushed me away and moved toward the passenger side of the car. "You're not having a baby? How do you know for sure?"

"Because my period came on, Perry. You want to see all the gory details? I can show you the pad. I got it on." She started unbuttoning her pants.

"Alright, girl, why you got to be so nasty? I'm just asking. You had a brotha worrying for weeks. You could have told me the moment your cycle came on."

"It just came on this morning! I'm not trying to keep anything from you. We can't say the same for you, though."

"Well, you thought she was your friend. She came on to me the day we had our triple-date thing. I didn't want to throw that all up in your face. I knew you wanted close girlfriends."

"But, I also asked you what you thought. You could have told me she was no good for me."

"Savoy, we've been there and done that. You're high school friend really hurt you. I didn't want you to be hurt again."

"Well, that's why you have to let me go."

"What do you mean?"

"I am not strong enough for a high-profile boyfriend like you. I'm starting to second-guess myself, thinking I'm not pretty enough or funny enough. What if I don't have sex with you again? Will you leave me? After this scare, part of me never wants to have intercourse ever again in my life."

"Alright, you didn't have to tell me all of that," I joked, completely understanding where she was coming from.

"I don't know, Perry. You just think I'm supposed to be strong enough to understand. Most of these females on this campus, if given the opportunity, would take you in a heartbeat. They'd love to have you as their guy, and I just can't handle that. One day, I might do something wrong, and one of them can console you in a way that I can't. Make you feel good in ways that I am just not ready to anymore. I know it's wrong for me to just prolong this. The truth is, the fact of the matter is . . . I want out."

Then she opened the door and got out before I could say anything. We weren't far from her place, but we weren't close either. However, maybe her cutting it off was best. I just put my head on the steering wheel and thanked God I wasn't going to be a father. The whole relationship thing with Savoy was now in His hands. I couldn't stress over it. I watched her walk straight to her door, and took off.

The weekend was here again. It was an open weekend on the football schedule. I was glad because this weekend off was a chance to give my weary bones a rest before the next big game. My parents came and swooped me up, giving me a break from Atlanta. We were headed to Athens, to one of Georgia's home games, to see my sister throw down on the cheerleading squad. Before we got into town, we stopped at a restaurant.

When my mom went to the ladies' room, my dad said, "So, you've been moping the whole ride up here. What's up? Your girlfriend left you?"

"Naw, see, why you gotta call me out like that?"

"So, is that what happened?" He looked completely clueless.

"I don't know, Dad," I said as I looked over the menu. "I think I'm just too young to deal with all that girlfriend stuff."

"I know you care about the young lady, but I'm a man. You know I know sometimes one woman isn't enough."

He was eluding to the fact that I found him cheating on my mom a while back. Though it really ticked me off then that my mom wasn't enough for him, I now understood that it was really hard when a woman makes it easy. Most men are dogs. With all the whining women do at times trying to keep brothers under their thumb, it's no wonder.

"But frankly, son, I like the girl. Most of the girls out here want to hook up with you and have your baby or something. She doesn't strike me as that type." He had no idea how close we had come to messing up in that area. "Plus, sometimes you just need a friend to talk to, and men just can't talk to each other. Girls are good for us."

"So what you saying, Dad? You want me to be tied down?"

"Well, if you look at it like that, of course not. But you trying to act like you don't care." He hit me in the chest. "I can see you do. At least be friends. The same drama she's giving you, the rest of 'em probably gonna be worse. One thing I can say for your sister, she and Tad been off and on for the last two years up here at Georgia. First, I wasn't for it at all, but I know she has someone up here that cares about her a lot. That Tad boy is going to make sure my baby is alright. You my son, and I treat you a little tougher, but in reality, you're my baby, too. Women just know how to take care of us. You might not need it right now from this girl, but don't get flax out here and have your peter in every Sally, Sue, and Jane."

"Dad!"

"Come on, boy. You trying to be a man? We can talk real, right?"

"Naw, it ain't even about all of that."

"I'm just saying."

"I hear you, I hear you," I said, fully getting his message.

We were at the Georgia game, and of course, Georgia had to be winning. Being a Tech guy, I hated that. But for Dakari, my old high school teammate, and Tad and my sister, I was there to support the home team. As long as we beat them at the end of the season, I'd be cool. My dad went down to say hello to his girl, and my mom and I stayed seated.

One Bulldog fan in front of us said, "Excuse me. You look like that Skky boy from Tech."

Now, I didn't have on any Tech paraphernalia. Best believe, I certainly wasn't wearing no red and black either.

"Yep, that's my son," my mom proudly stated. "My daughter's a Georgia girl, though, so don't throw anything at us."

"We won't." The man and his friends were a little drunk and joked among themselves. They turned around, and he said, "We wish you were on our team."

"Don't look like you need me," I said just as Tad got the ball and ran it for a touchdown.

My mom said, "Look, you know if we invite you somewhere, you can invite Savoy anytime you want."

I didn't say anything. I just kept watching the game. She started squinting her eyes at me.

"Is there something wrong between you two?"

"Come on, Ma, we're watching the game."

"Well, I think you're too young to have a girlfriend anyway," she said, surprising me.

Excited, I said, "Really, Ma? You feel that way?"

"Yeah. Girls these days can put a lot of pressure on you. I try to tell your sister all the time to leave Tad alone and give him some space. I'm sure she doesn't listen. Needless to say, they are made for each other. But not everybody is like Tad. I don't think you're like that."

"What do you mean? You think I'm not ready for a serious relationship?"

"Exactly!"

"Ma, I'm not trying to play the field or anything like that."

"No, you're not. You're trying to graduate on time from school and concentrate on your relationship with God. Something with a female can certainly be a distraction and provoke you to sin. A lot comes when a guy lays with a girl."

"Ma, tell me," I said, really wanting to get in the mind of a girl.

"It's not just a physical thing for a girl. Yes, it might feel good to some, but another big element of it is intimacy. The connection, the love the girl feels when she gives herself to a guy. If you don't know that you love her like that, it's best just to stay away. Not to mention the other risks that are involved."

"Yeah, I know about all of that, but I just don't understand why girls make it so serious. Nobody is married or anything."

"A female brought up the right way sees that part of her body as special. She wouldn't want to give it to anybody. The way I know Savoy, I'm sure she is, or *was*"—my mom looked at me and hit me on top of my head—"a virgin. I pray she still is." I looked away. "You can't cross that line with her and not expect her to have some type of ownership feeling toward you.

"Be that right or wrong, it's there, and it's not something she can just turn off," Ma continued. "I'm sure you got all them hussies up at that school wanting to lay up with you. That could be a lot of pressure for a young lady to hold it all together."

"Well, she broke up with me. She told me she couldn't handle it."

"And that is what is best until you can understand where she is coming from. Just enjoy college without all of the strings attached. You've got enough demands from your coach, and from your dad and me for those grades to be right."

"Ma, it ain't like y'all are paying."

"Boy, whatever. Don't get stupid. We don't want you to fail out and we then do have to pay."

"I'm just playing, Ma, I'm just playing."

"Seriously, son, would you want some guy to be with your sister, make her feel like she is the only one, and then be only half into it? Lead her on, take advances from other girls, call sometimes, not call others, deal with her when he wants to?"

"No," I uttered.

"Then there you go. Then you need to keep your little peewee to yourself until you're ready to accept all that the Lord says a godly relationship is supposed to be. I'm not telling you what you can and can't do. You're a grown man. I do know you're still a little wet behind the ears. You get out there, start laying down, screwing around, and come up with all kinds of diseases. Girls pregnant. Somebody else accusing you of rape. You know, son, been there, done that. I'm not laying down the law. I'm just laying down facts."

# ~ 6 ~
## Spiraling into Trouble

Practice got a little rough when one of the defensive linemen, Dedric, came over and smashed Mario to the ground. Mario lay there for a minute. The hit fired up the defense. The players on the other side of the ball were cheering. Mario sprang back to his feet and wanted to hit somebody. He looked behind him and saw that no one on offense had his back.

"What's wrong with y'all? They cream me like that, and y'all think it's funny or something. No one's gonna do anything. That's why we can't get long drives off the ground on game day. The press got the nerve to be on my inconsistencies. What do they expect when I have no blocking?"

Shark, the left tackle who hardly ever says a word, exclaimed, "Mario, you don't need to blame us for stepping outside of the pocket. We've tried to protect you all season long, and you do your own dumb moves, acting like a one-man show."

Coach Red got in between the two of them and said some words I dare not repeat. And Coach was a Christian man, so for him to cuss, he was fed up with the foolishness. Mario pitched a fit, throwing the football down, kicking up dirt, and jerking away from the coach, but he went into the locker room and had a meeting with the offensive coordinator. Coach called the rest of us into the middle of the field.

"Listen," Coach Red said, "we're a team. Offense is going to make some stupid plays sometimes. Defense is going to miss some plays also. Special teams might not keep up its end either. But if we all play to the best of our abilities and don't point fingers, we can carry each other and maybe even carry each other to a title."

"Yeah, right, Coach. We lost a game. You're talking about next year, right?" Dedric yelled out.

"No, I'm talking about this year. Just like we lost, everybody else is capable of losing, too. And since we have a loss, we may be underestimated by our opponents. If that's the case, and we play like a team, anything is possible. Certainly remember to pump each other up. There's going to be enough people ganging up on us trying to tear us apart, we don't need to destroy ourselves. Do what you need to do to lift up your teammates so we can get ready for Saturday's game. If you don't feel we can win a championship this year, then keep your tail at home."

He was the color of his name, red as fire, and he charged us all. But I needed to know what I was going to do with my information about Mario.

Lance came over to me in the locker room and said, "I'm sick of this. The whole team knows something's up with him. If you're too chicken to rat him out, then I will. I'll handle this."

I grabbed him by the back of his jersey and pulled him to me. "Look, I don't want any beef with you, but this is my score to settle. I brought the information to you. You were only working on a hunch of some kind. Let me talk to him, and don't ever call me a punk again." I shoved him.

Mario was in a Jacuzzi, with the one beside him empty. I didn't know how I was going to approach the subject, but I needed to find a way. Though I didn't want to admit it to Lance, he was sort of right. I was a little afraid to talk to Mario about everything I felt. But a great man pushes past his fears. I was a team player. I wanted the team to win.

I said, "Hey yo, Mario?"

"Dang, man, can I relax in the tub? You rookies always trying to talk to us about something."

"Freshmen, man, freshmen."

He fanned me away. "Whatever. What do you want? I can't even relax now."

"You said a couple of things to me. . . ."

"What you want?" he screamed, cutting me off.

As anger rose in me, I said, "You betting on our games?"

He rose up out of that Jacuzzi like I imagined Lazarus did from the grave back in the old days. He came over to me and placed his hands around my neck. The problem was that he miscalculated my power.

"Wait, wait. Hold up, man," I said, pushing him up off me as I raised out of the Jacuzzi I was in. "I asked you a question. You didn't need to come at me."

He walked toward the door. "I don't owe you no explanation."

Dripping wet from my waist down, I stood in front of the door so he could not leave. "Yeah, you do owe me something."

"No, trust me, I don't owe you anything. You don't know what you're talking about."

"I know what I saw."

"What do you mean, you saw? You need to drop this."

"What you trying to say, Mario?"

"Perry, you may be young, but you're not dumb. Whatever you think you saw, you think I'd be in it only for a dollar or two? Dudes I deal with are past crazy. You feel me?"

At that moment, I drew my hands up. I remember back in high school, my boy Damarius fought back a dealer for his loot. I got roughed up for trying to get the middle of it. I wasn't going down that route again. I was in a pickle—a bumped-up sour situation. As much as I didn't want him to be betting on our games, I wasn't going to rat him out. My life was too valuable to me, and although I was trying to be completely finished with all of this information that I knew to be true, I wasn't ready to write my own death ticket.

"Pretend like we never had this conversation," he said, grabbing a towel. "Just be on your game, and whatever I have to do won't affect you. You feel me?"

I nodded. I moved completely out of his way. I had enough drama; the last thing I needed was more. He left the training room. It might not have been right to keep this to myself, but it was definitely smart.

"I think I'm going to flunk out of here," Deuce said to me, holding his head with his shaky hand.

He looked more out of place than a fish out of water. Midterms were in a couple of days. The brutal academic routine was more challenging than the football field. It was easy to see that maybe this tough institution was the wrong choice for a lot of guys.

See, in recruiting, no one lied. We were all told repeatedly that the academics weren't going to be easy. I really believe a good number of the players felt that if they produced on the football field, all else would be taken care of. That might be true at some schools, but at this school, it didn't work like that.

"You'll be fine," I said to my friend, not sure really if he could cut it.

"You think so?" he asked as he pulled out two pieces of paper from his calculus class with Fs on them.

"Those are just quizzes. This is a midterm. You can turn everything around if you just make the grade."

"If I knew the quizzes, I wouldn't be stressing about the midterm. Can't you see I don't have the concept?"

"Yeah, yeah, man, but you've been in here studying every day this week. You haven't even been pulling your duty at the crib in cleaning because you've been in here studying."

To share the chores, we created a calendar showing whose turn it was to do what. Deuce's chores went undone. Lance, Collin, and I divided his up because we wanted him to work on the books.

He broke down. "I shouldn't have even come to Tech. I was just an average student in high school."

"If you can remember all those offensive plays, we can break down this math," I said, letting him know he was intelligent.

"Naw, I'm not smart like you."

"Boy, please," I said to him. "Let's go study."

"Really?"

"You can tell me what areas you are having trouble in. I'll walk you through it. We'll get through this. When I was down this summer, you didn't let me wallow. You made sure I got back out there and did it. We'll work this math thing out until you get it."

We slapped hands and walked out. I was all ready to study. I figured there was no better place to crack the books than the library. However, as soon as we walked into the packed place, we had eyes staring us down. It seemed our fellow students were in awe of two freshmen football players. People waved and smiled.

"See, this is why I can't ever concentrate," Deuce admitted. "You got to talk to the fans."

"Boy, you better come on and find a corner so we can start this studying."

"I'm coming, I'm coming." Then Mr. Social left me.

He wasn't the only one with distractions. As I sat down

and looked up, I found Charlie in my face. I was surprised that she was in the library. She had on sweats and a lot less makeup than usual. She looked real cute, like a person here to learn, not some hooker in a nightclub. But I still was quite ticked with the girl.

"What's up?" she said seductively.

Nonchalantly, I said, "I'm studying."

"I just came over to say hi. You can take a minute."

Now she was going to tell me what I could do? That's where girls went wrong. A girl with a little spunk was cool. The girl that was too sassy, with a mouth too big for her own good, needed to go sit down somewhere. Instead of letting myself get reeled in and allow her to control the situation, I ignored her.

"Oh, so it's like that?" She made a few more teasing re- marks.

I finally said, "Look, let me just be honest. You were friends with my girl and . . ."

"Wait, let me stop you. I know you and Savoy are broken up. It's not my fault your girl is so insecure. Or should I say your ex-girl?" She laughed.

My face showed a guy who was fed up. Charlie needed to quit while she was ahead. Her pushiness was borderline trashy.

"Okay, okay," she said, leaning down toward my ear. "What- ever it was that you liked from Savoy, give me a chance and I can triple it."

Before I could say, "No thanks, I'm not interested," Deuce walked over to Jailyn. He was way too interested in her legs to be reeled back in to what we actually came here for. I couldn't believe he was so off-focus.

"Sit down, Jailyn," Deuce said as he pulled out a chair for her.

I don't know what he was trying to do. Impress her or what? I could now see why his grades were slipping. He had no desire to stay on task.

"Boy, we here to study," I said to him.

"They're studying, too. Charlie, go get your stuff."

"Cool," she said, happy to get an invitation. I could have taken all his books and mine, and whacked him upside the head. How stupid of him to invite Charlie over. He knew I had a girlfriend. I hadn't announced to the world we were done, but apparently Savoy wasn't following that same rule if Charlie knew. When Charlie went to get her stuff, Jailyn indicated for me to come close.

I bent in, and Jailyn said, "Savoy is here, you know."

No, I didn't know that. I swallowed hard. Part of me wanted to get up and find her. I looked around. Jailyn must have sensed what I was thinking, as she looked around as well.

Jailyn shocked me by saying, "She's over there."

She pointed to an isolated corner. Savoy was laughing along with a preppy-looking Caucasian guy. She didn't look like she missed me at all.

In anger, I said to Deuce, "Look, I came here to help you study. You want to socialize, then that's on you. I'm headed home. I'm tired." I grabbed my stuff.

Charlie came back over to our table and said, "Where you going?"

She grabbed my arm. I yanked it away and walked away. Before I got to my ride, Deuce was beside me.

"Dang, man. You didn't have to get all hot and bothered. All you had to do was say it."

"I tried to tell you before, I shouldn't be the one trying to keep you focused on you getting your work done."

We drove home in silence. When we both got to our

place, we were shocked to see the front door wide open. Things were scattered in the family room. Deuce and I rushed in.

Deuce found Lance bent over on the kitchen floor. "Lance, what's going on?"

Lance breathed heavily. "Perry, they came here."

Blood was streaming from his nose down onto his chest. There was a lot of it. He was holding his ribs. His eye was messed up as well.

"What happened?" Deuce asked him.

Lance raised his head, looked at me, and said, "I couldn't let Mario get over on the team like that and not say something."

"You told the coach?" I said, looking at him angrily.

"Naw, I just mentioned something to him, and later I got a few visitors. Guess it's the goons that work for the bookie. They're trying to shut me up."

"Well, hopefully, you got the point," Deuce said. "I didn't know this was that serious, Perry. He's working with something illegal, man. What do you think?"

"It ain't fun and games," I said, frustrated.

"Ouch." Lance moaned as he bent over in pain.

Deuce said, "You got to go see the trainer."

Lance shot back, "And tell him what? I got the point. I just needed to find a way around this. I can't go see anybody."

"You should have just let me handle it," I yelled at Lance.

Lance responded, "You ain't doing nothing. So obviously, my way is working better than yours."

I said, "It didn't get us beat up."

"Hey, come on now. We need to stick together. This is a big mess," Deuce said.

It was a mess alright. One I did not know how to fix. Day by day, Mario's situation was worsening.

\* \* \*

Saturday was here, another game day. Having a week off made me excited about our game at home against our ACC rivals, the North Carolina Tar Heels. It had been a grueling week.

Thank God, I had gotten through midterms without too much worry. However, I couldn't say the same for Deuce. He felt like he didn't do well. All I could tell him was to get up and get ready for the next part of the semester. While Deuce was beaten up mentally, Lance was beaten up physically. As he groaned more and more around the crib, we tried to get him to see the trainer. Collin even told him he needed treatment, but Lance refused to go. As many fights as I had been in over the last couple of years, I had learned to play doctor for myself. So I helped patch up Lance, and he toughened it up to make sure he could suit up for the game.

Before we left the locker room, Coach gathered us together and said, "Listen, in order to succeed in life, you have got to believe in a cause worth winning. Right now, we're three and one. We have no losses in the conference. The Tar Heels have a good new coach, and two of the top recruiting classes in recent years. They have come into our house to take the sting out of the bee. Keep your eye on the prize. Stay alert. Don't slip and think we got this in the bag before we even get out there to compete. On paper, you might be better than them. But as we already know, the game of football is about heart and who shows up on game day to showcase their skills. Let's go cream 'em." Everybody put their hands in the center and repeated, *"Let's go win!"*

I didn't get out of the locker room before Coach Red said, "Skky, come here, son."

"Yes, sir," I said, and headed in the opposite direction from my teammates, who went out to warmup.

"I want to set up a conference with you next week."

"Yeah, Coach, sure," I said, trying to be the model player.

"I don't want you trying to pacify me, giving me short little answers. Something serious is going on in that apartment of yours."

"I don't know what you mean, Coach?"

"You don't think I've seen my backup quarterback looking like he's just come from a bar fight?"

"Oh, Lance, sir? Just a couple of nicks."

"So, you know exactly what happened to him?"

"Oh, oh no, Coach. No!"

"Skky, you're not a good liar."

"I'm really not thinking about that right now, Coach. I'm thinking about that speech you just gave. I want to get on the field and win this thing." I looked as serious as I possibly could.

Coach paused. He stared me up and down. I knew the buzz words. Though he cared about us as people, he certainly wanted to win.

"Alright, well, you get out there and get your head into the game. We'll talk next week. Something is going on, and I don't like it. You boys are here to play football and get an education. I'm sure I'm going to have to answer to his parents today when they see his eye. He's not saying anything. Deuce is not saying anything. Poor Collin Cox is all nervous."

"Yes, sir, Coach, we can talk next week."

"Alright then. Get out of here."

I was about to leave the locker room when I saw Collin taking his time tying up his cleats. I went over and sat down by him.

"Talk to me, man," I said.

"I just feel sick to my stomach. I've got an eerie feeling about this game."

"What are you talking about, Collin?" I said, frustrated by the fact that he had been down for so long.

Sensing my aggravation, he said, "Forget it, never mind. I can't do it. If something happens to Rick, I'm not going to be ready."

"Nothing's going to happen."

I don't know why I said that like I had a crystal ball and could read the future. However, I needed my friend to get up off his tail. He needed to feel empowered so he could get out there and kick the pigskin through the uprights.

On the opening play, our kicker, Rick, sent the ball into the air toward the Tar Heels. All our men missed the return man, and the only person left between the Tar Heels and the goal post was our kicker. Rick threw himself into the middle of the play and sprained his ankle. All I could do was frantically look around the sidelines for Collin.

What had I done? I told him he wasn't going to have to go in there. Now his number was certainly going to be called. How could I convince him that he could do it?

I prayed: *Lord, I put my foot in my mouth. Here I am thinking I'm doing the right thing calming his nerves, and now Collin has got to play. Help!*

The Tar Heels scored first because they were so close to the goal line. When we got the ball, Deuce ran it down to their twelve-yard line. When it was time for the extra point, too many players were in my way. I couldn't make it to Collin to give him an encouraging word.

I just clutched my hand and thought, *Lord, You've got him.*

The ball looked like it was going right in between the uprights. However, it went a little to the left. The crowd was stunned silent. Now the score was Tar Heels 7, Tech 6.

The second half of the game became a defensive battle. When our defense got our offense back on the field and it was time for us to drive, my number was called. I had no confidence in what Mario was going to do. But when he threw it short, I read his eyes and his arm, and I ran up and shook a defender off. I caught the ball. Then I went an extra thirty-seven yards for the touchdown. The crowd went wild. It was exuberating. Everything was falling into place. We were now leading 12 to 7. I passed Collin when I was walking off the field. He was walking on for the extra point.

"You can do this," I said to him with passion.

He just stared at me blankly. If he didn't believe in himself, he was going to miss it. Unfortunately, he missed it by a lot. This time it was too low. The crowd booed. Thankfully, time ran out, and we won the game anyway.

I ran up to Collin and said, "It's okay, man. You'll get 'em next time. With Rick having a sprained ankle, we're going to need you next week."

"I don't even want to do this anymore, Perry. I never should have listened to you anyway. I knew I was going to have to play today. I knew it."

"Dang, man, you suck," an offensive lineman said as he walked past Collin.

Then Lenard, our big-mouthed wide receiver, said, "We'd better get another kicker in here. The way you're playing, I could do better. You a wimp, man."

"I'll show you a wimp. I'll kill you. I'll kill you!" Collin yelled as he charged the wide receiver.

I had to pull the two apart. The crowd, which was leaving, turned around and stopped to watch. Collin was always so reserved. I had never seen this side of him. He just snapped. Thank God he didn't have a weapon in his hand because there was no telling what he would have done with it at that moment.

"Man, you go talk to somebody," I said to him.

He went under the bleachers and fell to the ground. "What's happening to me, Perry? What's happening to me?"

Collin started shaking. I knew that at this point he was way beyond being helped by a positive word. I had to find the trainer. Everything was spiraling into trouble.

# ~ 7 ~

# Covering My Faults

Okay, let me not kid myself. I'm walking to class, and every girl I see from behind is appealing to me. I appreciate the tightness in the flat behinds. The ones that jiggle are nice, too. And the plump bottoms make you want to grab 'em.

Honestly, I didn't know what was happening to me. When I slowed down and women passed by me, their perfume made my head spin. My eyes started undressing all the girls. It was like I was some sex fiend or something. What in the world was wrong with me?

Most of my life, I've been so focused on athletics and academics that I've been able to keep out the female species in a way that was over the top. You know, brothers just trying to be out there, get their groove on, and stick it in anything with legs. That was just never my MO. But now, if one of these girls rubbed me, I might be willing to skip class and handle the urge.

What did that say about me as a person? I felt I had no kind of decency. Certainly, I didn't seem like a guy trying to allow the Lord to lead in his life. So, I did the only thing I could do.

I prayed: *Father, for real, I've got some issues, some demons in my mind that I didn't even realize were there.*

*Now that I've opened the door of sexual temptation, more
to get me in trouble is coming my way. I can't close this
door. I need Your help.*

"Hey, sexy, there you are," Charlie said, coming up to me.

*Okay, Lord, didn't You hear me ask for help?* I thought,
looking up at the sky.

It was a brisk October morning. Though she had on a
sweater, the V came down almost to her belly button. It was
too obvious that my eyes were roaming, taking in the view.

Charlie batted her big pretty eyes. "If you want me to take
it off, all you need to do is say so. We can skip class and enjoy
each other."

I cleared my throat, as if she had completely misread my
demeanor. "What are you talking about?" I looked the opposite way.

She took her finger and moved my chin back toward her
face. She stuck her finger in her mouth and then let it slide
from her lips to her chin. Her hand enticingly moved down
her throat, then slid down her chest.

"Come on," I said to her, "what you doing?"

She winked. "Just an appetizer. This is the meal I can tell
you want. Girls talk about the way I dress, saying I'm a little
too provocative. Or they say I go around flaunting this and
that. Trust me, I know men. My dad schooled me a long time
ago."

"I don't know what you mean," I said, picking up the pace
to get to class when I noticed my watch said it was five minutes to the time calculus was going to start.

"You don't know what I mean? Every man wants what they
think they can't have. And just because I dress this way doesn't
mean I come on to every brother out there. That's what Saxon's
problem is. He tipped us off to his sister because he wanted
some of this, but why should I settle for a puppy when I can
have the Saint Bernard, you know?"

As I tried to walk faster, I forgot that Charlie ran track, too. She was able to keep up, and she had my same class. I wasn't going to be able to shake her. I was going to have to talk to her. I wasn't attracted to her mind or to her heart, but I certainly was starting to feel her in a way I couldn't explain.

Again, I mentally said, *Lord, didn't You hear me ask for help?*

The temptation she was throwing in my face made me feel like I had asked Satan to give me a hand or something. That slime was happy to oblige. Trouble was written all over her body. Yet, as I looked at her lips, I could see myself getting a rise out of her if our tongues met. I couldn't even look down at the rest of her body.

Knowing that my thoughts weren't pleasing to God, I just said, "I'm gonna go to the men's room before class."

She got on her tippy toes, touched me on my shoulder, pulled me down, and said into my ear, "I won't bite, Perry. I just want to have a good time with you. There's no sin in that."

Did she know I was struggling to try to please the Lord? Well, she was crafty, sneaky, and sly enough to say whatever she could to try to get a rise out of me. Either way, she had me pegged. I didn't like that one bit. I felt like I was on the football field lying on my back after taking the worst hit from a lineman that I had ever received—completely helpless. I didn't want to be that way at all. Thankfully, when I got in class, I was able to grab a seat in the back, and right before the professor dismissed us, I took off.

I was never really excited about having a one-on-one with Coach Red. But this time, it gave me a reason to make sure I didn't tarry, because if Charlie caught up with me, I might get kicked off the team for missing the meeting. Just thinking about the potential between the two of us got me excited.

As I entered the athletic complex, I ran into the chaplain. "You look stressed," he said.

"Yeah, I gotta go meet Coach." The chaplain never liked to put pressure on us, but I knew he was disappointed that I hadn't been to the FCA meetings or Bible study. Obviously he could tell I didn't have it all together. So just being honest, I said, "Look, I'm sorry I haven't been at the meetings and everything."

"You don't have to apologize to me, man. It's your faith. You have to take care of it."

"Maybe that's the thing. I'm seeing right now that just praying ain't enough. I'm starting to think things that are totally not in my character, thoughts the Lord wouldn't approve of. I just don't understand what's going on. Can we get a one-on-one session?"

"Yeah, you know I'm here for you anytime. But you need to understand that the devil is real. He's here to kill, steal, and destroy. I'm not telling you to go around giving him more time than he needs. By no means do you need to think he's out there coming for you. You got a lot on the ball. As a freshman, you're our hottest player. I've seen you on TV giving the Lord the glory for what's going on in your life. You think that makes Satan happy? He was up in heaven trying to run stuff."

"I got you," I laughed.

"You've got to be able to put on the full armor of God. That's praying. That's being in His word. That's believing that He's got you. That is knowing that Satan can't touch you. And that is knowing that sometimes you are going to go through some things that will make you tougher. When temptations come, don't hide and try to battle the enemy on your own, but seek God's refuge, a'ight?"

I nodded. I realized that I definitely was under severe spiritual attack. I could only hope that I was going to be able to handle it.

*   *   *

"I'm listening, Perry. Spill it," Coach said as he got in my face while I sat in his office.

He wanted me to tell him what was going on with the teammates I roomed with. I wasn't a snitch. I couldn't do his job for him. If he wanted to ask me about my faults or what was weighing me down, then we could have some dialogue. So I sat there biting my lip and twiddling my thumbs. I didn't realize my actions were ticking him off more.

He hit his desk, walked to my other side, and yelled, "Why has Collin's kicking gone to hell? And why was Lance beaten and bruised? And why is Deuce doing everything but studying. I don't understand, Perry. What's going on in that apartment of yours? You boys partying every night? You guys up there on drugs? You guys think y'all own the Playboy mansion or something—girls running in and out of your pad? Talk to me. Talk to me now!"

Honesty or loyalty—what did the Bible call for in this kind of situation? Then I thought about what the chaplain said. The devil is out and about. He wants me to screw up. Truth always reigns. I just needed to be careful about what I said so that I could also be loyal. I didn't want to mess anybody up.

"Coach, you don't have to worry about drugs, or alcohol, or girls running in and out of our place. There's nothing like that going on up there. Really."

He sat down in his big leather chair. I didn't spend much time in his office, so I was amazed by all the awards and plaques he had displayed around the place. They included an MVP trophy that he had gotten back in the day, a couple of college championships, and even a Superbowl ring, displayed in a case.

"Looking at all my stuff, huh?" he said, catching me.

Unable to deny it, I replied, "Yeah. You had one heck of a career. Actually, you're still having that, you know, Coach?"

"Yeah, I'm trying to get you guys to the championship

game, but not just *to* it—I want you to *win* it. But you have to taste it. You all have to stay focused, and you each have to help your teammates stay strong. I know you're a believer, and in the Bible, it talks about being your brother's keeper. I don't want you thinking that telling me what's going on with your roommates, or with any other member of this team, would be selling out."

I looked at him in a strange way. My eyebrows rose. My lips curled. I couldn't believe he was so cool sometimes.

He sensed that and said, "Yeah. Oh, but I'm still down, and if you don't explain to me all that's going on, then you need to step it up and really be a leader. Keep those guys accountable."

"Coach, I got my own issues," I told him, being completely transparent.

"I know that. I know it's got to be a lot of pressure on you. Your grades are good and you're performing on the field. You haven't dropped the ball. Well, not since that first game, against USC, when you lost it for us." I figured he would not let that go. "But son, sometimes we have things happen in life that we can't erase. Sure, we can forgive, but can we forget? I don't think we're supposed to forget the things that brought us down. The reason I have all these things in my office is because I learned from my shortcomings. I tried to get better than them. I tried to conquer my demons. I listened to those who were in authority and had my best interest at heart. I took their advice, made it my own, and succeeded. I helped those around me be the best they could be. Football is not a one-man sport. Got me?"

"Yes, sir."

"Well, then, act like you know what I'm saying. Help your teammates get the same winning edge you've achieved. Make sure you don't lose it yourself. Ain't nothing wrong with being the good guy, the star, or the hero. Great men are

those who know how to use their influence. You get what
I'm saying?"

"Yes, Coach."

"Then get out of here."

I was eating a little later than normal because of the meeting I'd just had with Coach Red. The track girls were in the
café we shared. Actually, I saw everyone but Savoy. I tried not
to wonder where she was. We were over; why should I care?
But when I sat down alone and Charlie took her plate up
from a table clear across the other side of the room and came
and sat by me, I realized her visit would bring me more trouble.

"I know you're not afraid to have a little female company."
Charlie winked.

"I just don't think it's best that we do this here, you
know?"

"Okay, I'll leave if you promise to take me out tomorrow.
Remember what I told you earlier. I won't bite."

She picked up some carrot soufflé, placed it in her mouth,
and gave me a little show that made me wish tomorrow was
today. Just when I smiled, Savoy walked into the room and
saw the two of us.

Charlie leaned toward me and said, "To keep folks out of
our business, why don't I just meet you at the Varsity?"

"You just want hot dogs?" I teased, knowing she had more
expensive taste than that.

"Ah, the things I could do with hot dogs. If you're a good
boy, maybe I'll show you." She made me real hot.

The next day came. We were eating together again when I
felt her hand touch my knee. She scooted her chair around
to me. I realized this wasn't really what I wanted. However,
another part of my anatomy disagreed as her hand rose toward my inner thigh.

When we finished eating, we drove to an empty parking lot near the Dome. We began making out. Her kisses were so aggressive, she almost bit my tongue. She called it nibbling, and it was quite irritating. When she reached and unbuttoned my pants, I jerked away.

"Charlie, you're hot and . . . I'm sorry."

"No, you're not gonna tell me you're sorry. You're not gonna tell me you don't want this. Come here, boy," she said, pulling on my shirt.

The look of sadness and disappointment on Savoy's face the day before when she saw us in the cafeteria tore at my core. What was I doing? Why wasn't I fighting for what mattered to me? Why was I making my bed even worse?

I started up the car. "I'm gonna take you home now."

"How dare you humiliate me like this, Perry! You may be good at football, but you're not some god. You can't just treat me any kind of way. I'm not a slave or machine you turn on and off. You wanted me, but now you don't want to deliver? Why'd you even get me all worked up? Whatever happens next is all your fault."

*Whatever*, I thought, as I drove in silence. Lust was sin, and though I had some issues to work out, she couldn't bring me down any lower than I was, degrading myself. When she got out and slammed the door, I realized I had to quit making stupid mistakes.

"Why are you calling me?" Savoy yelled at me when I phoned her from my Virginia hotel room to say hello the night before the game. "We haven't spoken in a while, and every time I see you, you're with some different chick. You trying to call me to ease your conscience? You might as well hang up right now."

"Wait, wait, don't be like that," I said. "I don't know who you saw me with, but I remember seeing you once in the library. If I recall, you were laughing it up during your study session with a dude."

"Perry, we're not attached. There's no need for you to criticize me. There's no need for me to talk about you. Honestly."

"Well, you brought it up, Savoy."

Okay, great, let's hang up. We can't talk," she said. "Goodbye."

I said, "Please! I just wanted to see how you were. I miss you."

"Perry, Saxon's on the team with you. My brother tells me over and over and over how much you are into only yourself. So don't try to feed me any bull about missing me because I'm not buying it. I don't want it, and if you force it on me, I'll throw it up. Okay?"

"Saxon and I, you already know, are like oil and vinegar. We don't mix. I'm not saying he's lying about me—"

"So then he's telling the truth."

"No, I'm not saying that because I don't want to say anything negative about your brother."

"Oh, Perry, please stop with these excuses, okay? We're through. We're finished. You don't have any claim on me. You miss me. I think about you sometimes. But we tried it twice. It didn't work either time. So, I'm sorry. There's no need to try to fix what's irreparably broken." Then she hung up.

I couldn't believe I was lying in my bed stressing out about a female, but she had always been such a good friend, too—a voice of reason when I was confused, a calm voice when I needed one, an encouraging voice. I just wanted to hear from her, but she wasn't down for that and I had to step back and respect it. I had to move on. So I talked to the one person I knew would listen.

I prayed: *Lord, I told You so many times that I'm not per-*

*fect. You can see all I do, and know that I have many flaws.*
*I just need You to help me work through some of this. Do the*
*right thing more times than I do the wrong stuff. Help me,*
*Lord, to model myself after You daily. I just want to be bet-*
*ter. Amen.*

The next day, as I was dressing in the locker room, Mario
came over to me and said, "Hey, can I talk to you for a sec?" It
felt weird when the shoe was on the other foot. I knew how
Savoy felt when I called her up. Heck naw, I didn't want to
talk to Mario. The brother was betting on our games. What
could he and I have to talk about? He sends goons to beat up
my roommate. Though I didn't have the balls to rat him out,
I certainly wasn't punk enough to let him think I was down
with his plan, so I just walked away.

I didn't even realize Mario was following me until he
came around in my face and said, "Alright, alright, I owe you
tons of apologies. You kept your word. You kept your mouth
shut."

"Man, please. We ain't gotta be friends in this thing," I said
to him, trying to end the conversation. "No need to smooth
anything out between us. Mario, it is what it is."

"I just wanted to let you know that today, I'm supposed to
win big, so I'm gonna be throwing the ball your way, you
know? We're on the same team today."

"Whatever you say, man, because that's always my agenda.
Do your thing, and I'll do mine." I walked around him.

I couldn't stand to look at his face anymore. Yeah, he
seemed disappointed and even bummed out by himself. I
knew from firsthand experience with my boy Damarius that
once you began working with a thug or crook, you got in
deeper, and sometimes you couldn't get yourself out of the
mess. That wasn't my fault. He dragged our whole team into
it, and if anyone ever learned what I knew, our whole season
could be in jeopardy. Again, I didn't have time for it. I wanted

to try to find Collin before the game, to give him some encouragement. Our kicker was still out with a sprained ankle and Collin had to come through this time, but I couldn't find him. When offense scored on Deuce's two-yard run, Collin lined up to kick. I jogged off the field, giving him a thumbs up as I passed, but he didn't look at me, and for some reason, I felt sick to my stomach. When his kick went wide right, not through the uprights, I knew he hadn't found his zone. I had no idea why Collin had this funky playing spell.

All through the summer, the boy had been bad. He almost took the starting position from the jump. But now he had the freshman jitters or something.

In the second half of the game, his first field goal was also a miss. The score was 6 to 7 with Virginia winning, and because this was another ACC Coastal game, we wanted to win. When we lined up, Mario called out my number. I caught the ball and took us down to the ten-yard line. On the next play, he called out Lenard's number. Lenard and I did what we needed to do in practice, but we still weren't speaking. Yeah, he was an upperclassman. Yeah, he thought he had earned my respect. But he was jealous of me, and I was tired of kissing his tail. The route he was supposed to run would bring him over to my side of the field, but when he got tripped by a defender, I caught the ball. I scored the winning touchdown without any extra points from Collin.

Instantly, Lenard came up to me and said, "I'm sick and tired of your showboating. I had it. I could have gotten back up and caught the ball."

"Whatever, man. You didn't. Don't get up in my face when you're mad about me playing a position better than you ever could."

He pushed me right in front of the media. Coach was furious on the sideline. I know we still had ten seconds in the game, but Lenard couldn't punk me like that. I wasn't gonna do nothing. When he pushed me back a little, I couldn't believe how angry I got. I charged him, and we were practically wrestling in the end zone. As we rolled around in the grass, I felt a lot of thoughts race through my mind. I had gotten so far away from my walk with the Lord. Lust had entered my brain, and now anger. Though I had been talking to God about my weaknesses, I needed help. I needed to do more than covering my faults.

# ~ 8 ~

# Discovering Dark Days

My fists just started drilling Lenard in the face. I was in such a trance, I didn't even realize his helmet was off. Tons of lights started flashing in my face, and then a voice brought me back to reality.

Deuce said, "Come on, man, stop! Stop hitting him, man. A'ight."

As soon as I let up, Lenard kicked me in my chest. He knocked me back a couple of feet. Our position coach, Coach Sanders, got in between the two of us and escorted us off the field to our locker room. Not only did I have a cut in my chest, but I was also saddened by my intolerable behavior.

"I'ma press charges! I'ma press charges!" Lenard said, charging in my face.

Coach Sanders replied, "Lenard, both of you insulted the other. It's on tape that you threw the first punch. I hope Coach Red or the NCAA doesn't put you both off the squad completely."

I think at that moment, our outlandish behavior sank in for both of us. We might have messed ourselves up for good. Although I loved the game of football, and the thought of not playing it made my stomach churn, knowing that I could get so angry that I couldn't even control it scared me. Lenard's eye was swollen and his nose was bloody. I had messed him up in a rage. I knew the game was over because we could hear the rest of the players celebrating on the other side of the locker room. Lenard, Coach Sanders, and I were cramped in a small space, waiting on the coach.

"Coach Sanders, I need some treatment," Lenard whined.

"Hold your hot head back," the coach told Lenard.

As we waited, I silently prayed: *Lord, there's no way I can explain my actions to myself. I strongly dislike Lenard, but I didn't think I hated him enough to practically bash his head in. What makes matters even worse, Lord, is that I don't even remember some of the conversation. I don't recall the situation or some of the confrontation. Am I that messed up? Am I so far gone that there's no way You can even help me?*

Deep into my prayer, I rolled my eyes and shook my head as if the answer was no, I was a lost cause, a person even the Lord would turn away. But Lenard saw me and misread my gestures, and suddenly started squealing on me.

"Oh, Coach, see? He ain't through. Why I gotta just sit here? He's rolling his eyes at me and stuff. What's up, Perry? Bring it, bring it!" He motioned for me to try to take him.

"Coach, I'm upset with myself right now. This ain't even toward him no more."

"Cool down, Perry. And Lenard, settle down so your nose can stop bleeding."

Finally Coach Red entered the room, but he wasn't alone. My father and Lenard's uncle were with him. I had embarrassed my family. My dad looked agitated. I took a towel and placed it over my eyes.

"Naw, son," Coach Red said, "I want to see you. I want both you boys to look at me. I brought your families here so that they could see how disgusted I am with your behavior.

We're a team on track to win the ACC and possibly more. We're all of like mind. But then you two go out and make a childish display of yourselves! It'll be on *Sports Center* all week."

"I'm just tired of his showboating, Coach," Lenard muttered.

His uncle popped him across the head. Lenard's aunt and uncle, like my folks, went to road games. I'd chatted with his uncle, and I wished Lenard had half his heart. He needed something to shake him up and let him know he couldn't rule the world.

"Boy, you've been jealous of this boy since before he got here!" Lenard looked at his uncle like a pleading, pouting kindergartener. "Naw, I'm telling it, 'cause ever since your dad died when you were two, my wife and I have taken care of you like you were our own kid. We'd do anything for you. But you need to stand now and learn from your stupidity. You're hotheaded sometimes. If you ain't the one in the spotlight, you get upset. That's just not how the game of football is supposed to be played, son."

"Yeah, but—" Lenard said.

Coach Sanders said, "You hush up, and give some respect to your uncle. That's my problem. I haven't been as tough on this team like I needed to be."

Lenard's uncle continued, "I'm just saying, the defenders took you out of the play. What's wrong with Perry coming across the field and making the catch?"

"I know what's wrong with him," my father cut in. "My son catches the ball, and he runs straight up to Lenard to taunt him. Instead of taking a knee and being thankful, Perry showboats."

"I was just happy, Dad. That's all," I said.

"Yeah, but the two of you guys getting into an altercation makes your coach look bad, Perry. It actually negates all the good stuff you've done here this year. Y'all looked like two animals out there," my father said. "And especially two black boys. No disrespect, Coach."

"No, none taken. Get 'em straight. That's why I want y'all in here," Coach Red said.

Lenard's uncle said, "Yeah, people expect black football players to be thugs. As much as you all have got going for yourselves, you just proved that theory right. If I tell you nothing else, remember that character is what truly builds a man. Lenard, I taught you better, boy."

"Yeah, I'm sorry. Sorry, Coach," Lenard said.

My dad stared me down. I apologized as well. Lenard and I shook hands, but I knew it would take a miracle for us to be friends.

"Well, guys," Coach Red said as he saw our gesture, "the problem is, I don't know how much pleading I'm gonna have to do to the NCAA to let you guys still play. It's a tough situation. It can't be erased with a little apology. Two of my leaders practically throwing their futures away. It's a real sad moment for me as a coach, truthfully."

Coach Red went out and gave Coach Sanders some instructions. He came back in and asked Lenard and his uncle to follow him to get medical treatment. I was instructed to come in fifteen minutes to get checked out. Physically, I knew, I would be okay. It was the gash in my heart that hurt. How could I even look my father in the eye? He had taught me how to be a man, how to be political, how to never let my true feelings get me into trouble. And for nineteen years, his plan had worked.

Of course, I felt worse when he said, "Son, you've always been a good kid for me."

"Did it look bad out there, Dad?"

"It looked like you just lost your mind. I want to know what's going on with you. What's got you so crazed that you could continue hitting on a man like that? He wasn't threatening your life. What was it that made you snap?"

"I don't know, Dad, honestly I don't. I can't even remember most of it."

"Are you serious?"

"Yeah. I mean, maybe I need to see a shrink or something," I said, tears welling up.

He came over and placed his hand on my shoulder. We hadn't had the most affectionate father-son relationship. However, at that moment, I could tell he really wanted to understand what had gotten to me.

In a sincere voice, he said, "I've pulled back in your life, son. I'm trying to give you some space, trying to let you grow and be a man. Have I been wrong? Do you need me more? 'Cause you have a dad to talk to. You don't have to carry the weight of the world on your shoulders. You are still my child. Understand?"

"Yeah, I do, Dad. I can't put my finger on it. It's not just one thing. I am fed up with a lot, and I have a lot of pressure on me. I'm not saying I'm ready to give up football or anything like that, but—" I just hung my head low.

"Well, you know there are gonna be consequences, and you're gonna have to get yourself together so you can deal with them."

"Yeah, I made a crazy bed. I'll lie in it."

"I know you feel low right now, but you gotta use this moment to make yourself stronger."

"Yes, sir," I said as I stood up and hugged him.

It was really weird. I woke up with Savoy weighing heavily on my mind. And it's not like I didn't have enough things to worry about. We were right in the middle of football season, and I might not be able to play. Word from the NCAA still hadn't come down. I had been badly dissed in the press.

Also, I ended up getting stitches thanks to Lenard's cleat spike going through my chest. Even with all that, the girl who had cut me loose, and rightfully so, wouldn't leave my brain.

I tried calling her, but got her voicemail. So I said, "Savoy, hey, I know I'm not your favorite person, but I'm trying to reach out to you. Hit me back when you can."

Minutes later, my phone rang, and I assumed she was hitting me back. "Hey, girl."

"Girl? This ya boy, Cole. Dang, man, you've been in school way too long. You better check that caller ID."

"Hey . . . boy, what's up?"

"Nothing, man. I just wanted to make sure you were alright. See if you need to talk. I saw that brutal massacre. You pumping that boy's face straight into the green. Dang, man, if I didn't know, I could have sworn you were Damarius or something."

"You've talked to him?" I said, not proud of the analogy.

"Naw, the three of us have gotta do better."

"So how's it going in Columbia?" I asked him, knowing he was in the middle of football season for the South Carolina Gamecocks.

"Man, for real, I ain't wanna talk about me." Cole stopped talking and seemed to be distracted. "Wait, turn on your TV. I just saw the ruling come across the ESPN wire."

"What?" I said.

All of a sudden, Lance busted into my room. "Hey, man! You're only out one game!"

"Guess you gave me the news too slowly," I said to Cole, laughing.

Cole said, "That's good, though, man. Only one game."

I was thrilled. I knew I got off easy.

"You don't need me to get a crew and come down there to take care of that boy, do you?" Cole said.

"Naw, man. I'm done with all that."

"Alright then," he said, closing the subject. "So what honey did you think I was?"

"It's weird, Cole. Savoy and I haven't really been working out, but I woke up with her on my mind, you know?"

"And you just thought she called you? What you got—EPP, TSP, ESP, or whatever it's called?"

"No, boy. I just called her before you called me. I thought she was hitting me back, that's all."

"Oh, okay. You really think something is wrong with her?"

"Naw, nothing like that."

"You might just wanna get your groove on."

"Boy, you crazy."

"I'ma let you go, man, but for real. If you need to talk, or anything like that, you know I'm here, right?"

"Yeah, man, I know you're there."

"A'ight, dog," he said before we hung up.

Good friends can always make a dark day brighter. I really appreciated Cole caring about me beyond our high school years. I knew he'd be there for me always, and it just felt good that he cared enough to let me know I was in his heart.

When I couldn't shake Savoy from my mind, I tried her again later that day. I dialed her as I headed up to see Coach Red to get the official word on my playing status. I got her answering machine again. I hated that I had to go see Coach and put on a diplomatic face. With today's technology—the Internet, newspapers, stuff just going all across the wires—I already knew what he was gonna tell me. Of course, as I thought, he dragged out giving me the information, making me think I wouldn't play ever again.

"So, you do understand how severe all this is?" he asked. "Or do I need to assign you to some counseling?"

"I'm gonna hang out with the chaplain some."

"Yeah, I suggest you do that. We all have issues, son. We all have things that weigh us down. But we can't act half-cocked."

"Yes, sir," I said.

"Well, the Lord must have been working on your side. I guess the NCAA, is going to suspend you guys for only one game. I need you to help get Saxon ready."

"Yes, sir, Coach."

"Get on up, and get outta my office. Boy, if you ever need to talk and get things off your chest, reach out with your mouth. Don't use your hands."

I nodded. When I went down to the locker room, Deuce came up to me and said, "You know, Lenard's been in here bragging."

"Bragging 'bout what? The fact that we only got a one-game suspension?"

"No man . . . he's taking Savoy out." Deuce stood ready to figuratively catch me.

"What?" I said, as if that news had to be a lie.

What in the world would she want to go out with that joker for? She wasn't my girl, but she *was* my girl. Whatever he wanted, he didn't mean her any good. As soon as I stepped out of the facility, I dialed her number again. I was angry when I got her voicemail. I got in my car and drove over to her apartment. Nobody answered the door. Of course, on my way out of the building, I bumped into Charlie. She tried to put her hand on my face.

I jerked away. "I don't have time for this right now. I'm looking for Savoy."

"Jailyn told me she was out with another football player. She's moving on. I don't understand why it's so hard for you to do the same."

I just threw up my hands. I didn't need to get into an argument. I drove around the campus for an hour looking for the two of them. I didn't have Lenard's cell phone number, and I certainly didn't want it. As it started getting dark, I felt my stomach churning. Then my cell rang, and I looked at it. It was Savoy.

"Hey. You alright?"

"Perry . . . you've gotta come get me. He dumped me out on the side of the road somewhere in downtown Atlanta, and it's scary down here."

I said, "Where are you?"

"I don't know." She panicked.

"Okay, you've gotta calm down," I told her, really irritated and somewhat upset at myself that I hadn't finished Lenard off.

How dare he take out his frustrations on her! If he still had issues with me, then we needed to resolve those man-to-man. Thirty minutes later, I found her near the Georgia Dome in a dark parking lot. Her sweater was ripped in the front. I jumped out of my car and rushed to her. She fell into my arms.

"He told me you needed me. It didn't make sense when he said we were going to see you and my brother. Then he drove to this parking lot and said y'all ain't coming. Before I knew it, he had his hand down my pants, and . . ."

Madder than a person who'd just lost his child to senseless gang violence, I said, "We gotta go report this."

"No, we can't. Please." she pulled on my shirt.

"He threatened to hurt you and Sax if I said anything. Plus, I don't wanna be the scandal at this school. I'm trying to run track, make national and possibly the Olympics. I just can't deal with a press nightmare. I just can't believe I was so stupid!"

When I touched her shoulder, she screamed and went

over to the passenger side of the car. I didn't know what to do. She would no longer let me comfort her, and she wouldn't allow me to take her to the police, so we just sat there.

Just as the sun was gone from the sky, hope seemed to have dimmed in both our lives. The only thing I knew for sure was why Savoy had been so strongly on my mind. She and I were connected, and I had to believe that God would help both of us have brighter days again. But was that realistic?

It was the homecoming game. Though we weren't playing an ACC rival, the win could help propel us toward a national championship berth. I detested the fact that I had to sit in the stands. Of course, I liked being there to support my teammates, but not being allowed to be on the field and physically contribute was a career low point. It was one thing not to play because of an injury. It was still another to be sidelined because the coach chose to go with a different player. It was just embarrassing to be sitting beside my dad due to an NCAA suspension.

My dad knew I was bummed and said, "Son, it's no reason to look sad. You might as well shake this up and put it behind you. You'll play next week. When you get out there, make it count. For now, cheer your team on."

What he was saying made sense. What good was a pity party gonna do me? But I was really tired of always having something negative going on.

Spiritually exhausted, I silently said: *Lord, show me how to make You proud. Show me how . . . to be happy. Whatever I'm doing is not working.*

And as soon as the game started, it was like the Lord jumped on my problem because I wasn't focused on myself anymore. I was up on my feet, cheering like every other true Yellow Jacket around me. The punt that Collin kicked gave the opposing team the ball on the fifty-yard line. It was a terrible move, and he got lots of boos. Thankfully, our defense was up to the test. They had only three plays, and they were turning it over to our offense. We weren't so unfortunate on the kick return either. The ball got placed on the twelve-yard line.

At the first snap, Mario handed it off to Deuce. My boy cut to the left and then broke into a smooth run straight between two defenders. When he got into their secondary, he did a reverse on a defensive back that made the guy miss. Deuce was off to the races. We had 6 points just like that.

"What's up with your roommate coming into the game with his head all down?" my dad said as he pointed at Collin, who was jogging onto the field to attempt the extra point.

Shucks, I had to put my head down, too. I didn't even want to see the kick. I had no confidence in my suite mate. Sure enough, when I heard more boos, I knew he missed it.

"Dang it!" I said. "I'm worried about him, Dad."

"Yeah, I'm worried about what kinda damage he's going to do to y'all. If y'all didn't have a heck of an offense, relying on him, we certainly wouldn't win any games."

"Yeah, he just mentally hasn't been all there. His door at home is always locked. He never wants to talk about anything. Dad, I say I'm worried because I understand how keeping it all bottled up inside only blows up eventually."

"Speaking of blowing up," Dad said, "have you and Lenard talked any more?"

"Don't even mention his name to me, Dad."

"Son, you gotta get that under control. You guys are both playing the same position. You're going to have to see each other in practices. Thankfully, you're getting another chance on the football field. You can't allow him to screw up your future. You know what I'm saying?"

"Dad, he's got such character issues. He plays so low and dirty. It goes way beyond what you know."

"Well, tell me. If it's such a bad situation, then explain it to me. Break it down."

I just shook my head and watched Deuce score another touchdown. My dad didn't need to be all up in that.

When the game was over, I was the first one in the locker room, to find Deuce and congratulate him. That done, I looked for Collin, to console him for another horrific performance. He did hit one extra point, but he missed two field goals and the first extra point in the game. I heard from Deuce that when Collin was coming into the locker room during halftime, a fan tossed beer cans at him.

Though I had been there for Savoy this past week, she asked for a little space. I was still thinking about her, but all I could do now was leave it all in God's hands. Certainly, if He was able to help me, He could help her, too. When we got home that evening after the homecoming parties, hanging out with our parents, Deuce celebrating with the press, and all, we heard the sound the phone makes when it is off the hook coming from the other side of the apartment. Deuce and I looked at Lance.

"Can you put your phone back on the hook, man? That's loud," Deuce said.

"I didn't know I left it off the hook. Let me go put it back on, because I want the press to be able to get through if they need to chat with you, boy," Lance said to Deuce. "Man, you jammed."

"What's up?" I asked when Lance came out of his room and shook his head, indicating that it wasn't his phone making the irritating sound. "Whose phone is off the hook then?"

"It's coming from Collin's room. And his door is locked." Lance knocked on Collin's door and got no answer.

Deuce said, "We gotta do something about this. That boy knows not to leave his door locked. But I got the jammy."

Deuce went into his room and came out with a wire

hanger. He played with the lock for a bit, but when he finally opened it, all three of us panicked. Collin lay sprawled out over the bed with half his body hanging to the floor. An empty pill bottle was right beside his pale hand.

"We can't just stand here. Somebody's got to check him. What if he's dead?" Lance shrieked.

I found a faint pulse, but when I hit him a couple of times and got no response, I became frightened. What had the pressures of non-performance caused our buddy? Life as a college athlete was extremely demanding, but it was never supposed to be so overwhelming that it made you want to take your own life.

"I'm calling nine-one-one right now," I said and got up to get my cell.

"*Wake up, man!*" Deuce shouted.

As soon as I got an operator on the line, I handed the phone to Lance for him to explain and to give directions to where we were. I could only pray over my feeble friend's body and hope we hadn't gotten there too late. Growing up certainly meant taking the good with the bad. This was another low. I felt like I just could not take any more despair. I hated discovering dark days.

# ~ 9 ~

## Restoring Perfect Order

"**I** think we got here a little too late," one of the paramedics said to his partner as they fervently tried to revive Collin.

"I got a pulse! For real, I felt a pulse not too long ago! He's gotta be okay!" I said in a panicked voice.

I started moving the paramedic closest to me out of the way. I had to do something. They seemed like they were giving up hope. Deuce and Lance reached in and pulled me back, though.

"Let them do their job, man," Lance said into my ear.

A paramedic agreed. "Yeah, he's right, sir. We need you guys to clear out of the room. We can't do our job if you're distracting us with your antics."

As my two roommates pushed me out into the hallway, I shouted, "Come on, Collin, man! You don't wanna check out of here now! We can get your life back on track. I'm sorry if I wasn't there for you. Come on! *Come on!*"

I fell to my knees as his bedroom door was slammed in my face. I needed God to save him. I remember how I felt when I lost a high school friend. Ciara was an eleventh grader with so much life ahead of her. Though I believed God knew what He was doing, I just wasn't ready to let another young life leave.

"Come on, man. Get up," Deuce said, as he tried to pick me up off the floor.

"Man, get back!" I said as I pushed his hand hard.

I looked across the room, and Lance had tears coming down his face. Though I desperately wanted to feel that kind of sadness, none would come. I just felt rage and anger. Why hadn't I been able to get through to Collin? Though he felt like he had the world on his shoulders, didn't he know that he also had three roommates who cared?

Lance came over and grabbed my hand. He gave Deuce a look, to join us. Deuce obliged and walked over to the two of us. We all held a tight grip.

In an upset tone, Lance said, "Lord, save our roommate. I'm sorry, Lord. He told me he wanted to talk to me the other day, and I was busy. I was moping and crying about what I didn't have, wanting to start, wishing I could showcase my skills like Perry and Deuce. So much into my own world that I didn't even realize I had a friend in trouble. Please don't let it be too late for Collin because of my selfishness. If I never see a day on the football field again, save his life. Please save his life!"

He couldn't even finish the prayer; he just broke down. When we cut loose our hands, I slammed mine on the wall. They opened up the door to his room and wheeled him out quickly.

"He's holding on," one of the paramedics said to the three of us.

"Can I ride with him?" Lance asked.

"Yeah, we have room for one. Can someone call his parents?"

"Yeah, I can do that," Deuce said.

Lance grabbed his jacket and shoes. Deuce started dialing his parents. I knew I had to call Coach.

"Perry, don't tell me you're in trouble, son. It's eleven thirty at night," Coach Red said groggily.

"No, sir, Coach, it's not me," I said, a little broken.

"Perry, what's wrong?" he said in a stern voice, understanding the severity of my call before I even said another word.

"It's Collin, sir. He took a whole bunch of painkillers." I paused. "It's not good, sir. They're rushing him out now to the hospital."

"Oh no, son, no!"

"Yes, sir, Coach."

"You hold on. I'll see you at the hospital."

"Yes, sir, Coach." I hung up the phone.

Saxon and his roommates came rushing into our apartment. They started drilling Deuce and me. This horrific tragedy brought us all together.

My dad was staying at his mom's house. I needed him now. This was hard.

I dialed him up, and he said, "Hold on, son, let me tell your grandma one thing. Mom, no, you are not going out tonight. It is too late!"

"Boy, I'm grown!" I heard my grandma yell in the background.

If I wasn't so down, they would almost be funny. I still couldn't believe she was living it up, but as I thought about Collin holding on to life, I realized my grandma knew a true secret. She was proof we had to live every moment to its fullest. In my opinion, I was now down for her getting her groove on.

"Mom, don't leave this house!" he yelled, but apparently she ignored him.

"Dad, Dad, Dad!" I said, trying to cut in.

"Yes, son, what's up?"

"Dad, you gotta meet me at the hospital."

"The hospital? What?" he screamed.

"Dad, calm down. It's not me."

"Alright, Perry, what's up? What's going on? You're scaring me, son."

"It's my suite mate Collin." Explaining the whole thing, I finally broke down. "I just felt like I should have been there for him more. I knew he was hurting, but I've been having so many of my own issues that I didn't give him space, you know? Something I wish people would have given me is not what he needed."

"It's okay, son. The Lord would not want you trying to blame yourself. I know you prayed for your friend. You gotta trust it, though. You can't control what's going on with somebody else. He knows, and He can make sure that the one you love is okay, too. Gosh, what am I saying? I'm sitting here trying to control my own mother. It's just that as I'm talking to you, I'm learning that . . . I must let her go. Trust that God's got her. Can you be okay to get to the hospital, son?"

"Yeah, me and Deuce are gonna go together."

"Alright, I'll see you guys there in a sec."

Saxon actually drove the two of us. When we entered the emergency room, cameras had already beaten us there. I hated how bad news traveled so fast. What should have been a place of healing was like a madhouse. I felt like the Hulk— a small man starting to bubble up and turn green and mean. I wanted to take one of those cameras and smash it in somebody's face. This was serious! This was personal. Thanks to the media, Collin already felt like a failure.

My dad rushed in, and looked at me and said, "Come on, son. We need to walk over here."

"No, Dad, I need to talk—"

"No, son, we need to walk over here." He just held me. I was a big ol' baby, feeling comfort in my dad's arms.

"Thanks for coming," I said.

"You're a good son, a good friend, and a good man. You care. God is going to honor that."

Coach Red came in at the same time that the doctors did. We all went over to a private corner, and the doctor said they had gotten Collin stable and pumped the pills out of his stomach. They couldn't promise us he'd completely pull through, but now we were at peace that he was okay.

Sunday morning, I was better, but still dressed. Though Collin was still in the hospital, he'd made it through the night. By now, word had gotten around to most of the team, and at our place, we had such support. Though we'd been winning since our opener, we hadn't really been acting as a unit. It was amazing how in the midst of tragedy, we began trying to really be there for one another.

Deuce knocked on my door. "Hey, man, you got company."

I had just gotten an opportunity to go to sleep at 7 a.m. It was now only two hours later. I wanted to scream out, "Not now!" but I realized, as Lance did the night before when he felt bad about not being there for Collin, that sometimes we have to give for people—be there for them. Put our own needs aside and be helpful.

"Sure, come on in."

"Are you decent?" the sweet, sexy voice of Savoy called out.

She was the last person I was expecting. Inwardly, I smiled, though. What a breath of fresh air she was.

She said, "I was bringing groceries to my brother's place, and he told me what happened to Collin. I wanted to come check on you and make sure you're okay. He wanted to take his life? Oh my gosh, Perry! I'm so sorry!"

I checked my breath. Though it wasn't as fresh as I'd have liked it to be, I wasn't going to offend her. I got out of bed and dressed in a T-shirt and shorts. I stood before her scratching my back. Though she was here to make me feel better, it felt kind of awkward. With everything going on, I just wanted to release all the tension built up inside of me. Throw her on my bed and just go for it. And I hated that I felt that way. She tried to ease the tension by giving me a big hug, but feeling my body next to hers was getting my mind into even more trouble.

Then she quickly brought me to reality by saying, "I didn't come to stay. I just wanted to let you know that I'll be praying for you guys over here. I heard it was a real hard night, and I wanted to let you know that if you need anything, I'm here."

"Oh, I'm cool. I'm good," I said, backing away from her.

"I know I pulled away from you, Perry, but you know how much I care. It's like, you were there for me when I called, and now I want to be here for you, too." I gave her a thumbs-up. It was corny, but it was safe.

When she left, I immediately headed to my shower and adjusted it to be as cold as possible. I needed to cool down. I was way too excited, and I didn't understand why I was getting myself into trouble—letting my desires control my mind. So I tried to be productive. I got out and checked on Deuce. He had already gone to sleep. But then I heard Lance laughing.

"What's so funny in there?" I said. He jumped up, and whatever he was listening to or looking at he tried to hide from me.

"What you doing, boy?" I said, completely intrigued.

"Oh, nothing, nothing, nothing. What's up with you? Collin's good. I'm good. You good, right?"

"I don't know, man."

"I thought you'd be in your room a little longer than you were," he teased. "I saw Savoy."

"That's just the thing. I'm really struggling to keep my hands to myself. It's like I'm a nympho or something, you know?"

"Well, I got a way that won't require you to physically go there and give yourself extra worries." He reached underneath his mattress. "Let me show you something. I got a hottie here that looks just like Savoy! You can fantasize about her. You can look at her. You can drool over her. . . ."

"What are you talking about?" I couldn't believe Lance was showing me a *Playboy* magazine. "Man, I don't look at them things. I didn't even know you did."

"Oh, come on, don't judge. Don't knock it 'til you try it. It's safe, fun entertainment. You said yourself you've been struggling—looking at Savoy, wishing and wanting. Well, here you don't have to imagine her with her clothes off. See, don't she look like her?"

I had to take a seat on his bed when I saw the girl, whose body was more elaborate than anything I had ever seen in person. "Man, I can't look at that," I said, pushing the magazine away.

"Here, you take it. That was last month's. I got another one right over here. She does look like Savoy, doesn't she?" he asked again.

I walked out of his room and couldn't believe I had the magazine in my hand. Though it was all rolled up, I still took it. What the heck did that say about me? When I got back to my room, I flung the magazine on my bed and sat down. I looked over at it, and I quickly looked away. I wanted to look at it. I wanted to pick it up. I wanted to comb every inch of that girl's body—take it in, soak it in, imagine it.

But another part of me just knew I couldn't. I was already battling my flesh. I certainly didn't need to give myself anything else to make it even more difficult. But then I rationalized: Looking at pictures *was* a safer choice. I couldn't get anybody pregnant. I didn't have to worry about any diseases. And I wouldn't have any mental attachments to anybody. So without any more thought, I leaned back and started reading from the beginning.

I was amazed at some of the different pictures and positions that captured my attention. I no longer felt guilt. As I let my desire take over, I felt only more pleasure. And when I came to the picture that looked like the girl that really had my heart, I couldn't control wanting to release all my pent-up frustrations. So using Vaseline and my hand, and the picture for additional arousal, moments later I satisfied my urge.

Heading to the bathroom to clean up, I felt the guilt finally rushing back. Though I truly believed I couldn't help myself, I wondered whether a few moments of ecstasy were worth the utter humiliation I now felt. I wanted to take the magazine and rip it to shreds. But it wasn't mine to do that to, and I felt too unworthy to fall on my knees and ask for forgiveness. I was just a complete wreck. My body started shaking. My heart started racing. I truly hated myself. How could I fix this?

Boy, did it feel good to be back on a plane, headed to a football game. With all the craziness in my life, just to get a break from the madness, be on the field, concentrate on the sport I loved, was like a slice of heaven. But no sooner had I begun to feel free of strife than Mario came and sat down beside me. The quarterback who had been hailed as a hero thanks to his performances in the last couple of games had a disturbed look on his face that tipped me to the fact that something was up.

Without even looking at him, I said, "I'm not helping you throw a game, Mario. Forget it, man."

"I know, I just needed somebody to talk to," he said, putting his head down. We had assigned seats, and Lance was supposed to sit near me.

Mario said, "Don't worry about your boy. We traded out. I need to talk to you, Perry. I'm not like you. I need you to help me figure this thing out. This is serious. They'll kill me!"

I couldn't take his problems on my shoulders. Didn't he know I had enough of my own? Why did everybody think my life was perfect? It was starting to really tick me off.

"What should I do?"

"Oh, come on, Mario. Don't ask me that stupid question."

"Didn't you just hear me? I told you—they don't play."

"Well, how did you get messed up with them in the first place?"

"I'm trying to think back to figure all that out, but I can't go backwards. They made it seem like easy dough. I don't come from rich parents like you."

I let out a deep sigh. I mean, I didn't feel like I was rich— I didn't have a hundred grand in my own account—but I wasn't from the projects either. And most of the athletes that I'd played with, especially the African American ones, truly were here for an opportunity to play in the big league. And because Mario was shorter than the average NFL player, and his quickness and ability to get out of the pocket weren't ideal for pro teams, he was starting to feel the pressure of doing whatever he needed to pad his pockets while he had the college spotlight. I wasn't too high and mighty that I couldn't understand, but I certainly wasn't gonna be a part of it.

"Look, man, I've done all I can. I mean, I ain't said nothing to nobody. But if you intentionally throw this game . . ." I said, before he leaned into my face and grabbed the collar of my sweater.

"What? What you gonna do? Don't try me. You saw what happened to Lance." I removed his hands from me and pushed him back to the window of the plane.

"Lance ain't me. I got people of my own. You don't know where I'm from."

"A'ight, a'ight, cool down, calm down, I'm just messing with you. Ain't nothing gonna happen to you. You know I won't let nothing happen to you."

"Whatever, Mario, man," I said, taking a deep breath on the inside. My bluff had succeeded. He was afraid of what I would do. But that was his issue to worry about. I had to get my head back on straight; I had to get back into game mode.

In reality, if Mario threw me crappy passes, I would do all I could to catch them. However, a wide receiver's success comes from the stability of his QB, so the cards truly were in his hands.

Right before we began to land, the Spirit had me turn to him and say, "Look, you really are a good guy. I know it ain't cool when you step into some stuff that stinks. If you ever decide you want to get out of that world, I'm here. But man, we're a team. We need you to be the leader that you are. Forget what the scouts say about your size and this and that. Just go on and do your thing. You still have a world of opportunity out there in football. Don't throw it away for some bookie. You're better than that."

The chaplain gave us a talk before the game. We were playing the mighty Terrapins who didn't have as good a record as we did. However, they were only one game behind us, so if they won, we'd be even in the ACC, and we certainly didn't want that. I had been to a few chapels at this point, and the atmosphere was usually a lot more lively—people were more excited, more charged, more ready to get out there and make something happen. Today we sat quietly, already looking defeated.

"We might as well get back on the plane and go home," the chaplain said. Everybody looked at him with expressions that said, "Dang, where is he coming from with that?"

"I'm serious," the chaplain said. You know, when you look like you don't care about the game and you act like you don't care about the game, you might as well pack it in and not play the daggone thing. Just forfeit. Give it to the Terrapins."

Someone shouted, "We're ready!"

"That's what I want to talk to you guys about today. You gotta fix your house first when you wanna get things back in order. So many of us can look at other people and be like, 'Can you help do this?' or 'It's his fault; I don't have that.' We don't ever wanna look within to see what we need to do to help the team succeed or to help get ourselves back on track."

That cut deeply for me. I wasn't in trouble with a bookie, and I hadn't just been released from the hospital after trying to kill myself, but I certainly had issues that were severe and mentally draining.

The chaplain continued, "In the New Testament, there's a story of an adulterous woman. Everybody was out there telling Jesus about her—all her faults and everything she had that wasn't right. They didn't understand why he wasn't all moved by trying to stone her until he said to them, 'Ye who is without sin casts the first stone.' I be hearing a lot of picking on this team—mad about fights, mad about players missing a play or not making a goal—and I'm just saying, I watch the film, and every single one of y'all could step it up a notch. You know what I'm saying? We have a better record than Maryland. They're trying to get to us. All we need to do is keep playing our game; keep being the best we can be, and daggone it, can't nobody touch us! You guys know I'm here for you. You know your coach is here, and your position coaches are, too. But it's gotta come a point in your life where you decide that you want to be man enough to step up and get yourself right. Not be selfish. Go the extra mile for your team. National championships are won through collective efforts. Now, do we need to pack it in today, or are y'all ready to get out there and kick their tail?"

Three and a half hours later, we were all celebrating. Mario threw balls that were on point. Deuce ran routes that were out of this world. I caught some stuff, and so did Lenard. Defense didn't let them score at all. We were on it. We laid down our personal agendas and played as a team. And it actually felt good restoring perfect order.

# ~ 10 ~

# Surviving Adversity's Test

"Heyy!" Deuce said to me as he woke me up at three in the morning. "Hey, man, get up." His breath reeked of alcohol.

"Dang, man, get off me," I yelled. "We got exams tomorrow."

"I'm ready to take 'em. Bring 'em on . . . bring 'em on," he said.

"Okay, man, for real, you need to go get some sleep."

"*Sleep!* All I need to do is hit the bottle one more time and I will have the magic potion to ace this thing. You want some?" He swung a bottle in the air.

The next thing I knew, I had liquor all over my back. I could have punched him in his face. The boy wasn't stupid, he was just drunk.

"*Lance!*" I screamed at the top of my lungs, needing assistance with this fool.

"Oh, what you gonna do? Tell the preacher's son on me? Well, I ain't related his white butt.

"Yeah, what's up?" Lance said, half asleep himself.

"Where'd he get this from?" I said, holding up the empty bottle.

"Give me that back," Deuce said, grabbing for it. "There is no mo' in here! Well, Perry, I need your car keys. I need to go to the store and get some more."

I said, "First of all, you aren't old enough to buy this."

"Yeah, right. I play ball; I can get whatever, whenever, however. Just give me the keys." He got up and started searching through the stuff on my dresser. He found the keys, but thankfully, Lance stood in the doorway.

"No, guy, you're not going anywhere with your drunk behind." Lance stuck his arm across the doorway.

"Boy, please, you don't understand. You and smarty pants don't get it. I need a little something to help me ace my test tomorrow." Deuce curled his lips into a frown.

"Naw, man, that ain't the way to do it, bro'," I said, grabbing my keys out of his hand.

Deuce got in my face and said, "You want to take my gin. You want to take yo' keys. What . . . what, you want to take my status away and get me kicked off the team so you can be the only one doing something?"

I couldn't believe he hit me with this crap. He'd better believe he was lucky that I knew he wasn't all there. But he needed to settle himself down because I wasn't about to take his junk.

Not backing down, I said, "Man, back up. Go on and sit down somewhere."

"Serious, serious, I ain't mean to be offensive, but I need something to help. I'm nervous as hell about this test. I'ma get thrown out of school. Sax will take me to get brew. Move, Lance, move out of my way."

I joined Lance. We had to form a barricade to get Deuce to calm down. This was crazy. I really needed rest because I had a big test myself, but I guess this was what friendship was all about. Lance and I knew we could have been there more for Collin. Now it seemed we were being tested again. Looking into Lance'e eyes, I knew he, too, was determined not to lose another roommate.

Who knew when I would need them there for me again.

Being a college athlete certainly wasn't easy. It was hard enough to learn the plays, but throwing the academics—especially the tough curriculum at Georgia Tech—on top made it just that much harder. The pressure wasn't for some people, and boy did I hate to see Deuce crack.

"Man, you got too much on the ball, and you know I can't be out there without you," I said, thinking maybe reverse psychology would help him understand how much I cared. He looked out of it, as if he was only half hearing me. I gave Lance the eye.

"Yeah, you know you're the best running back in the ACC. You could get the Heisman this year."

"Aw, for real, dog, you think?" He was coming around to our way of thinking, so we pumped him up for about twenty more minutes.

Eventually Deuce forgot all about getting more liquor. Neither Lance nor I knew how to make coffee, but thanks to our moms, we had some in our apartment, and after two bad tries, we came up with something. He needed to drink to sober himself up, but when he took the first gulp, he puked all over our kitchen floor.

"I can't take the test. I'm sick, I'm sick." He hauled out before hurling even more.

Lance and I both needed our rest so we could do our best on our exams. However, we were in it and had to make do. Lance grabbed the mop, and I grabbed the Clorox. Deuce was stretched out on the clean part of the floor.

"I don't understand some people," Lance confided.

"What, what do you mean? We fed him a lot of bull, but a lot of it I believe."

"Yeah, me, too. But, why would someone with so much going for him just not crack open a book and learn the material? We've got all kind of help here for us athletes. You can always ask the professor, and the teaching assistants are always ready to help. It just don't make sense. So many athletes throw away their futures because they're lazy. If Deuce put all of the energy into studying that he puts into being a powerful runner, that boy could bust out of here in three years. I just don't get it. I'd kill for his opportunity out on the field. He's about to flunk out of here and waste it all. Shoot, maybe if I were him, I'd get loaded, too."

"Man, don't say that."

"You're not angry, Perry. We're sitting here having to clean up his mess. Trying to get him ready for a test that he is probably going to fail anyway. Now we won't be fresh and ready for ours. I mean, I don't know. I signed up to be somebody's roommate, and I've been worried about Collin and all, but dang, I ain't nobody's parent."

"I hear you, and I understand how you feel. But you're a Christian and your father is a pastor. Doesn't it say somewhere in the Bible—I don't know where, but somewhere—that you are your brother's keeper?" Lance just looked at me. "You get on my nerves. He gets on my nerves. Even Collin got on my nerves. But I wish Collin was here so I could have another chance. Collin's not here, but you two are, and somehow, we are going to find a way to get through this tough crap. We can't take the test for him, but you and I have studied enough to give him the basics and help him pass. Maybe if we give him another go at the coffee and start drilling his behind, we can help. All we can do is what we can, and hope that we succeed. If we don't even try—not make an effort, not care about him—that's when we'll fail, you know?"

He nodded, and we began to hope our plan would work. After all, what were friends for? We had to be there through the tough times.

\* \* \*

We had been working hard the entire football season. Now, however, with still only one loss, we were on a mission to work as a collective body to get through each week and win a spot in the national championship game. True enough, we were a long way from that, and everybody was a little tired of the hard practices, but we had gotten through a test that I felt we aced, and I was excited to be out on the field to release my frustration. I couldn't wait to see Deuce, to get a feel for how he felt. When he gave me a thumbs-up, it was all I needed.

I thought, *Alright, Lord, thank you for pulling us through*.

Why did it seem that when things were going cool, something would come along to mess them up. Mario was walking my way. All I could do was stretch and pretend that I didn't see him.

"Hey, man, can I talk to you for a second?" He said, interrupting my warm-up.

"Trying to get ready for practice," I said.

"It won't take but a minute. For real, for real, I need your help on this one."

"What? I already told you how I feel about the whole helping-you-win-or-lose-on-the-whole-spreadsheet thing."

"Yeah, but what if I cut you in on the action?" he asked, moving closer to me and rubbing his fingers together, alluding to the fact that he'd pay me off.

"Man, don't even insult me with that crap."

"Aw, I forgot, your parents are loaded."

My folks had me on a budget, and my dad was trying to build a new business. It wasn't about dollars for me. It was about loyalty, and somehow he needed to understand that.

So, I just went ahead and asked him, "Have you ever played in a national championship game?"

"No."

"Does that even matter to you—playing in the big dance?"

"Yeah, it matters. That's my agenda. I'm not trying to lose the game. Again, I'm just trying to win by a certain margin. What's so wrong with that?"

"Every time I think you got it, you turn around and give me some excuse as to why you have to be a part of illegal activity."

"I mean, sometimes I don't even think you're real."

"What, because I got morals? Because I stand for something? Because I'm not going to let you get away with what I know is wrong? I learned a long time ago that sticks and stones are the only things that can break my bones. You know what I'm saying?"

"I told you, these people I'm dealing with are crazy."

"So leave me out of it."

"That's on you. I'll figure out a way to give you an offer you can't refuse." He walked away, and when I turned around, I found Lance looking at me with such disgust that I felt like dirt.

I said, "Okay, the conversation was not what you think."

"It doesn't matter what I think. It's not like you're man enough to do the right thing."

"What are you talking about, Lance? And mind your own business." I tried to walk away, but he grabbed my shoulder pad and yanked me back.

"Alright, you need to watch it. It's like you're scared of him, Perry," he said to me. "You talked all this game last night about being your brother's keeper and all, yet you won't back me up on this with the coach."

I rolled my eyes. I couldn't believe he was trying to back me in a corner and make me play by his rules. He had his own agenda. Lance was pissed that he wasn't the starting quarterback, and he was willing to do anything to make sure

Mario was out so he could be in. Although I had a lot of issues with Mario's foul schemes, the brother had an arm. Plus, even though Lance's school beat my school in the 4A championship game last year, this was college and I wasn't sure that a freshman QB could give us the best chance at going all the way. Yeah, I had confidence that he could play and that he was good as a backup, but I certainly wasn't going to work to get the man who had a proven track record removed from our team.

Lance, apparently sensing my answer, huffed, "What is it, Perry? You don't think I can play?"

"Man, I'm getting ready for practice. I don't need to be answering none of this stuff. Those boys are crazy. You tried to go up against Mario and got such a butt-whoopin' you should have been placed in the hospital."

"That's what I'm saying. If you had backed me up and gone to the coach with me, they wouldn't be able to whoop up on both of us. I was alone. I thought I could do it by myself, but I can't and I need your help. It's like you're doing your thing, and screw everybody else. If that's the way you see it, fine. If that's how you feel, I can't change it. I'm calling a spade a spade. But if it's like that, don't say crap to me at the house. If this is how you treat people you care about, scratch me off the list, 'cause like you said, I can get my stuff by myself. You ain't gonna have my back, ain't no need to stand in front of my face."

He walked away, and I just stood there. I wondered if what I had done was the wrong thing. Now I was going to have no peace in my house. I didn't agree with him. Lance had soul. He was cool as heck. It was so bad that he thought I betrayed him. I was his boy, and I did want to have his back, but that didn't mean I had to bend over backwards to oblige his every demand.

As much as he whined, however, I also realized that he was going to need me before I needed him. I had been in enough relationships to know that if we had something true, that if we could be boys for real, this would work itself out. If he could understand that he wasn't the only one entitled to an opinion, then we could be down. And if he couldn't, then to heck with him. I'd be okay losing him as a friend. It wouldn't kill me. I had been through worse.

Being on the road for an away game was supposed to be a chance for some solidarity. I'd been walking on eggshells around Lance at my place. We were not talking to each other. So I could not wait for the chance to relax in my room at the hotel in Miami before the big game against the Hurricanes. But when I came out of the bathroom brushing my teeth, my roommate, Deuce, was dressed like he was ready to go clubbing or something.

I looked at him like he'd absolutely lost his mind. "Our curfew is in twenty minutes."

"Aw, man, let's go out and have a little fun. You and I were both recruited by the Hurricanes. We know how alive this city is. Let's have a little fun. I'm going to have a little fun with the upperclassmen."

"Boy, don't let them trick you into getting into trouble. We got the same record as these jokers. We need our sleep."

"You need to loosen up, partner. I'm going to get my drink on."

"Deuce, man, what's up? You done turned into a lush?"

"I ain't a snob that looks down on other folks, though."

Shrugging my shoulders, I said, "Whatever, man. Do your thing."

"I'm here for curfew, and when that's over, I'm headed out with Mario."

"*Mario*," I said, absolutely interested again.

I wondered what Mario's slick behind was up to now. He couldn't use me as his little pawn, so now he was going to try to use Deuce.

"And don't be selling me no bull about him beating on games and stuff." I just bit my lip. I didn't know what to say. "I'm serious, Perry."

"Cool, man. Think what you want to think. Lose focus. It's on you now. I saved your butt once; I'm not doing it again."

"Oh, so it's like that? If he were throwing games, how could we have an almost-perfect record?"

"I don't need to explain anything to you. Do what you want to do, Deuce. Just understand that I don't need no friends—you, Lance, Mario. I'm here to play football, and as long as we play that right, I won't have any problems with anybody."

"So, if the coach comes, you gonna rat me out."

"That's a risk you take," I answered, not really answering.

"Well, whatever. I'm leaving."

"Yep, just be stupid."

"I ain't trying to have a beef with you."

"Deuce, Perry, y'all in there? Open up," one of the trainers said.

Deuce opened the door and said, "I'm getting ready for bed."

The trainer said, "Alright, man, I'm just checking."

Ten minutes later, my roommate was gone. Contrary to what I had told Deuce, I did need a friend. I wanted to talk to somebody, but I didn't want a lecture or anything, so I dialed up Savoy.

"Hey you!" she said in a pleasant tone.

"Hey, Savoy. Sorry to call you so late."

"No, it's Friday night. You guys made it safely there?"

"Yeah, cool. Saxon hasn't checked in yet?"

"He's hanging out somewhere. What's wrong?"

"I don't know. I wish I could tell you, but I can't even put it into words. I'm just not gelling with the folks here, you know? I never got along with your brother. You saw on TV a few weeks back that Lenard and I can't stand each other. Now the two roommates I have left I really detest too. I know you and I got issues, but . . ."

"You just want to talk?" she said, finishing my sentence.

"Yeah," I said pitifully.

"I understand. The girls on the track team annoy me to no end. If they ain't talking about some guy looking good in his spandex pants, then they're talking about somebody on the team. I mean, how can we have camaraderie when there is so much turmoil?"

"Exactly. How are we to play one of the toughest teams, in my opinion, in the conference. Miami is also trying to become ACC champion, and these jokers can't even stay focused. It's like the carrot is dangling right in front of them, and they're trying to go all over the world to find one. I don't know, maybe I chose the wrong school."

"I've been feeling like that, too, but if we both stand strong, I think I'll be proud of us. Though people might get on our nerves, and others may not know the Lord, we have to try and get them to know God."

"What do you mean, win them back? If our friends want to go crazy, I don't think the Lord would want us to walk with them. They might pull us down," I said.

"Yeah, maybe you're right. Perry, I don't know what to tell you. I know you have a big heart, but you're also stubborn, and as hard as you try to shut people out and act like you don't care, you'll risk it all. So whatever you're doing to push everyone away, stop looking at them, stop judging them, and stop blaming them. Maybe you should start checking on yourself. You're a good guy, but you don't want to spend your days alone."

"Maybe that's why I need you back in my life," I said, as I appreciated her telling me the tough stuff. "For right now, you need to take care of yourself."

"I just know that if there is no way I could be happy with myself, then there is no way I could be happy with you, Perry. Vice versa, you know?"

"Yeah, I got you," I said to her.

I got off of the phone with her and went to sleep. A few hours later, I was awaken by a bang on our door. It was Deuce, drunk again.

"Perry, let me in. I can't find my key, man. Come on, man!" I sprung out of bed and quickly opened the door. He fell into my arms. "You were right. That Mario ain't nothing but a scumbag. He asked me to help him. And he didn't ask me to run hard . . ."

And then he threw up. I was startled by another loud knock on the door. It was my position coach. I quickly turned on the shower and pushed Deuce into it.

Coach Sanders said, "What was that? People are saying noises are coming from your room."

"Aw, sir, I tripped. I was going to get some ice. My throat's hurting."

"Why is the water running? Somebody taking a shower?"

"It's Deuce. He sweats bad, and sometimes he gets up and showers off. He does that all the time at home. I'm just used to it. I thought it was normal," I said, trying to sound honest.

"Alright. Well, y'all get some sleep. Y'all got a big game to-morrow."

When I shut the door, I couldn't believe I had covered for

that chump. But as Savoy said, I cared. Friendships aren't always going to be easy. To have true relationships, you have to go through something. But relationships that mean something, no matter what it is, are able to sustain. They are the ones surviving adversity's test.

# ~ 11 ~

# Resisting Temptation's Draw

It was a great feeling to beat the Hurricanes 27 to 21. With all of our individual issues, we managed to get it together and win the game. In the locker room, Coach Red huddled us around.

He said, "One more under our belt, guys. We're taking the Atlantic Coast Conference by storm this year. I always knew we could do it. The papers, the commentators, and the opposition knew we were capable. But you guys have come out week after week and proven the Yellow Jackets are a force to be reckoned with. Another big week coming up, though, men. We're playing Virginia Tech, so I need you guys to stay focused and keep believing in yourselves. I want you to enjoy this win, but don't celebrate too long and don't celebrate too hard. I can't afford to lose any of you next weekend. Congratulations, and get ready for steaks on the plane."

We all roared. It took us a while to get on the bus because we had to talk to the media. With other Division I schools losing every week and us continuing to put check marks in the win column, our stock was going up around the nation. Folks were starting to believe we had a chance at the big game in January.

"Man, thanks for having my back." Deuce sat down beside me after we were up in the air.

I said, "I was mad as I-don't-know-what at you, but I guess I can't shake you."

He leaned back and confessed, "I could have broken that one run if I hadn't lost my energy. I'm messing myself up, Perry. I got issues, man, and I don't know how to deal with them."

Honestly, I wasn't a counselor, and I was dealing with my own demons. I wasn't trying to ignore him. I wasn't trying to give him false advice either.

All I knew to do was to say, "Man, you better pray or talk to the chaplain or something."

"Well, I think I'm going to do both of those, or I'm going to be so far gone, you ain't gonna be able to save me."

I patted him on the shoulder. It took a strong man to realize he had weaknesses, and if you looked at your weaknesses and tried to make them better, in the end you would be stronger. And wouldn't that be well worth a little self reflection? I wasn't trying to share all of my business, but I knew what I was telling him. I needed to follow my own advice, so there wasn't a better time than the present to say: "You know what, Lord? Thanks for getting me through. You've gifted me in so many different areas, it's hard to work all of this out. Help me, Lord, to be the man you want me to be. Help me to be one who flees from temptation. Help me want to please You."

When the plane landed back in Hotlanta, we got on our busses as usual and rode back to Tech escorted by the police. It was two in the morning and most of us were dozing, until we heard the screams coming from the largest student crowd gathered to congratulate us that I'd ever seen. I knew a lot of other colleges had stuff like that to congratulate their team after winning. My favorite was at Auburn University, where they would go to the middle of town and throw toilet tissue over trees. Though we weren't up to that level of commitment, I was really excited that my school cared enough to come out and let us know we had their support. When I got off the bus, folks were chanting my name. It was getting harder and harder to keep my ego in check. My cell phone rang, and it was Savoy. I didn't know if she was in the crowd or what.

Quickly I asked, "You're not in trouble or anything, are you?"

"No, no."

"Are you out here?"

"No, my brother just called me, and I know we talked yesterday, so I figured I'd just call you and tell you, Great game. That one play when you caught the ball with one arm is being shown over and over again. I saw Deuce congratulating you after your second touchdown, so I guess you two worked it out, huh?"

"Thanks to you letting me know I wasn't perfect either. I'm still keeping him around. I was headed back to my place, but I slept on the plane and on the bus. I'm not really tired. You down for some company for a minute?"

She agreed, and the next thing I knew, we were in her room. I had never shared her space, and although it was set up similar to mine, it was all girly and feminine. Boy, did she smell good. The little lace nightgown she had on outlined her body. It took everything I had not to take my fingers and cup her breasts like I do a football.

She wasn't saying anything, and I wasn't saying anything. We were just staring each other down, and maybe our eyes were saying enough. She wanted me in the worst way. I shared those sentiments, so when she touched my hand and rubbed it gently, I slid closer to her and put my lips on hers. It was slow and gentle at first, and then all of a sudden, the passion between the two of us became more and more intense. When her hand went down my pants, I knew I was in real trouble, but it felt so good. How in the heck could this be wrong? All I wanted to do was show her how much I missed her and make her feel as good as she was making me feel. I lifted up her silky garment and buried my head in her bosom. Then we kissed again, and I leaned her back on her bed. Things were feeling so great. Suddenly she yanked herself from underneath me and stood, grabbing her shirt to cover up her chest.

"What? I thought we both wanted this?"

"Oh gosh, Perry, I do. I hate myself because I want you so bad. But I love God more, and I promised Him that if He let me not be pregnant a couple months back, I wouldn't do this anymore with you. I just can't."

How could I be mad at those words? I had pledged practically the same words to God. We had to do what we had to do, and that was stop, so I got up and politely told her I'd see her later. She wanted me to stay, but until I cooled down, I had to get away from her. Dang.

It was Sunday evening. Coach had broken us into groups. He wanted the freshmen to mingle with the upperclassmen. As long as I wasn't with Lenard or Mario, I figured I would be okay. Little did I know, that hanging with two crazy defensive guys, Dedric and Ralph, would be one adventure I wasn't ready for.

"Crystal City," I said as we drove up to the nightclub with the outline of a lady's body. "Where are we going?"

Dedric said, "Come on now, boy, you from Georgia. Everybody's heard of Crystal City."

"Man, I ain't got no ID to get into a strip club," I said to Dedric, who was driving.

"Boy, I got this. They know me at the door, and everybody thinks you're the man. You ain't wimping up, are you?"

"Wimping up? Me?" I replied back in a tough way, knowing that I needed to defend myself. "No, I'm straight."

Dedric said, "Cool, 'cause Coach wants us to bond. We're gonna take you on our kind of ride, and it ain't no merry-go-round, you know? You need a lap dance, boy. You need to loosen up a little bit."

"Shoot, man, the way you're catching them one-armed passes." Ralph, the other defensive lineman said, "you need a good rubdown all over your body."

I couldn't believe I was following them. Back in high school, I watched a couple of adult videos, but I never actually thought I'd end up in this type of place—passing out dollars and stuff. What kind of guys even went to these joints? And what type of person was I turning into by not taking a stand and refusing to participate in their so-called bonding activity? Maybe I was a wimp not because I wouldn't go, but because I would.

The music was loud and the lights were low. Men were screaming and ladies were bare. I saw women dancing for money right before my eyes that made the magazines I was into look like comic books. This was the real deal. If I paid enough money, I could reach out and touch, and get completely satisfied. To heck with Savoy. She made her pledge to God. I wouldn't need her if I got with one of these ladies. I wouldn't have to please myself, and certainly there would be no emotional ties. It would just be wham, bam, and thank you. A hit-and-go. The thought of it was tempting.

"Come on, man. We need to get some money," Dedric said to me. "The teller's right over there. What are you drinking?"

"Naw, man, I don't drink."

"Boy, I'ma buy you a brew." Dedric popped me on the head. "You can't be up here with no Kool-Aid."

"Where do you sit?" I asked him.

"Up near the runway, where do you think? You see Ralph

up at the stage trying to give that hottie a five? It's the two chairs right beside him. Hold my spot," Dedric added.

I didn't even go and get any money. I just sat there, actually controlling all my urges for a while. Then Dedric went over to the MC, and the next thing I knew, he was calling my name out over the loudspeaker. Two girls came over and ushered me onstage. Most of the women looked in their mid-twenties. Then this girl who looked sort of sweet came out. She had on a cheerleading outfit and did a back bend that bared all right in front of me. How could I not rise to the occasion and want to take this further?

Ralph started yelling, "Do yo' thang. Do yo' thang!"

The cheerleader and I wound up in a closed private room. My loins were excited. She pushed me down in a chair.

Smiling, she said, "I'm Lexi." Then she locked the door and started to remove her outfit. This just wasn't fair. I was trying to do the right thing, trying to be a good boy, trying to walk the straight and narrow. But here I was, by no fault of my own, placed right in the middle of my desire.

"Your friends are taking care of this. I'm yours for thirty minutes," she said into my ear. I just put my head down.

I was struggling so bad and then I thought, *Lord, You gotta help*.

"Can we talk?" I asked, a part of me hating myself for not wanting to take this all the way.

"Did you say talk?" Lexi asked with a smile actually on her face. "We don't have to say anything. I'm ready. I may seem a little nervous because I haven't been doing this that long, but I can perform, and if you're a little nervous," she said, stepping toward me and swiping her index finger down the center of my chest, "I can relax you."

She was a cutie-pie, a short little red bone around five four with curves that worked. I just didn't know her.

I sat her on my lap and said, "You said you haven't been doing this for that long. How old are you?"

"Twenty-one."

"Why you do this, if you don't mind my asking?"

"Because I need the money, and it's an effortless gig for a lot of loot."

"No disrespect to you, but it just seems really demeaning."

"You can't have too many problems with it if you're here," she said, smirking.

"Yeah, I'm really screwed, but what does that have to do with you?"

"I don't know. I don't want to be judged," she said as she quickly jumped up.

I put my hands in the air and said, "Hey, I'm not trying to offend you. I'm just trying to tell you that I feel like you really don't want to do this, and at least tonight, you don't have to."

Then she started to cry. I didn't know her issues. I didn't know her story, why she felt that her only option was to sell her body. All of a sudden, she just started sharing that she was a single mom and that her boyfriend had dumped her after he found out. She said her parents disowned her because she had the baby. Not being able to go to college because she didn't have the funds was another concern. It was just one thing after another, and the only thing I could think to tell her was that God could show her a better way out. I said that although it might not be easy, if she trusted him, He could help get her a respectable job, and she would be able to take care of her baby and put herself through school.

"Men see me and all they want to do is get busy. I've been jerked around so many times, I might as well get paid for it, you know? At least, that is what I thought." She said mumbling, but I could tell, that she was listening to me. "I don't know, maybe I should apply for a couple of loans and see what's out there. I do feel relieved that I don't have to be with you now. Not that you're not sexy as all get-out."

I smiled. She gave me a sweet kiss on the cheek before we left the room.

I said, "This is between . . ."

She put her fingers on my lips. "Yep, *us*."

When we went back out to my boys, Dedric quickly asked, "So what's up? She got skills or what?"

"She's better than good."

"Thank you," she said before we parted.

"Alright, you two. I'm ready to go," I said. I was through being suckered. I was through playing around. I wasn't strong enough to keep refusing temptation, and now I recognized that I needed to do everything I could to keep myself out of harm's way. Not giving a rat's tail about what anybody thought as I walked toward the door, I smiled inwardly as I heard them complaining to me. They might not have wanted to, but we left.

The Hokies were supposed to come in and smash our tails. They had no losses. Everyone was expecting them to play Florida State in the ACC championship game a few weeks later, but the gold and white showed up and showed out. Tech was victorious, and this time it was the home team. The Hokies tried to dominate, shoving Mario all over the place. I knew the shoulder had folded and he had nowhere to go. This time he had no hidden agenda; we were just being defeated.

However, in the fourth quarter, we made a stand. We didn't cave any longer. In the locker room, Coach Red said, "You see what can happen when you look the enemy in the face and tell them you won't take it anymore? They won't be victorious. And you won't be pushed around. You slayed the giant! Men, we're on to something here now. Everybody's going to be gunning for us. We're ranked number five!" The locker room erupted.

When we lost to USC at the beginning of the season, we weren't ranked at all, and now we had climbed to being one of the elite in the nation. I had to stay focused. After the meetings and the media, I got dressed and went into the crowd to try to find my parents, but every other person stopped me. "Oh, Perry, can you sign this?" "Perry, you did good at that."

I appreciated all of the accolades, but I was tired and just wanted to chill. I was sort of worried about running into my parents. Anyway, my dad told me he had a surprise for me. That meant that some of my relatives were coming to the game. I knew my grandma and one of her new beaus weren't going to be the guests because my father said that he was trying not to let her new lifestyle bother him. I knew they weren't going to be double dating soon. Suddenly, I spotted my mom. She still looked sophisticated, even sporting my jersey.

"My baby—twenty-two catches, two hundred sixty yards, three touchdowns. Boy, you better give me the heads-up. Son, I would introduce you, but I think you know these guys." I turned around, rolling my eyes in my head, not really wanting to be social. I was pleasantly shocked to see my high school buddies, Damarius and Cole.

"South Carolina didn't have a game today?" I asked Cole.

"Off-week, buddy!"

Damarius just happened to be off that week, too. He was a defensive back at Fort Valley State, a historically black college about forty miles south of Atlanta.

"Y'all chumps could have told me y'all were coming," I said, overjoyed.

"We knew you'd be nervous trying to show off. We home-boys worked it out with your folks and let you do your thing."

"I rode with your folks," Cole said.

"And I drove up. I'm proud of you, man," Damarius said.

Being that I had a tough road dealing with the folks around me, I become choked up seeing those two. As far as siblings went, it was just Payton and me. But these two were as tight as brothers to me.

"We know you're hungry, son. We're going to take you guys to Ruth's Chris and get a big juicy steak. Will that work?" My dad patted me on the back.

"What time you gotta be back?" Damarius said.

I said, "No curfew tonight, man."

"Well, we gonna grub wit' yo' folks and, then we gonna have some fun," Damarius said, sneaking in a wink when my pops turned his head.

"Y'all gonna hang out," I told them quickly, not wanting to get into more trouble.

"Naw, we just gonna chill," Damarius said. "I want to show y'all my spot."

My parents were staying at the Embassy Suites, with the restaurant we were going to connected to it. My dad always stayed with his mother. I didn't want to ask why they weren't going to be there. My mom sensed the tenseness. She pulled me to the side at dinner and explained that even though my dad was trying to understand that his mom was a big girl, he was having a hard time.

"Aren't you proud of these young men?" my mom asked my dad.

"Yeah, I didn't think these knuckleheads were going to turn into anything, with all of the problems they were caus-ing. Especially this one here." My dad cut his eye to Damar-ius. "A squirrel can catch a nut every now and then."

After dinner, my dad dropped around four hundred dollars on the tab and tip. The whole trip down to Damarius's college town was full of comedy. No heavy conversation. Just boys being boys. Cole farting and not letting us roll down the window. Damarius's phone ringing nonstop, with a different girl's number showing on the caller ID every time. And them teasing me, asking if Savoy still had me henpecked.

"Boy, I just can't believe you and Brianna broke up."

"Boy, please, I'm in college now. There are too many hotties walking around Columbia, I had to break her heart."

"Y'all know Ciara is going to come and whoop both of y'all for leaving the little high school girls crying every night," Damarius said, eluding to his girl, who died at the beginning of the year.

Neither Cole nor I knew how to respond to that. Ciara had been tight with our old chicks. Damarius had taken her death really hard. It wasn't his fault that they had been arguing, but guilt had taken its toll on him. To be joking about her when a complete year hadn't even passed yet melted my soul. I wasn't praying enough for my friend. I knew that he would be okay, but it was as if God was taking care of him anyway. This made me feel better than any of the three touchdowns I scored earlier that day.

So although Damarius hadn't been on my mind constantly, he'd certainly never left my heart. He pulled into an abandoned parking lot and got out a little white joint, which he passed to Cole. I didn't even think; I just took it from Cole and put it to my lips. I missed the camaraderie. I missed the brotherhood. And not wanting to be counted out, I did something that I would never normally have done before. I took a little hit, let go of my worries, and tilted my head back. I was obviously unable to be resisting temptation's draw.

# ~ 12 ~

# Dealing with Much

Man, what are you doing?" Damarius said after leaning into the backseat of his car and snatching the joint out of my hand.

Cole reacted as well, saying, "Yeah, what in the heck are you doing?" Then he bopped me in the head.

Unfortunately, I began coughing. Why would they ask me such a stupid question. I was doing what they were doing. Couldn't they see that? I was also trying to ease my worries and get a little groove on. Neither understood.

So Cole remarked, "I was handing it to you to give to him because I couldn't take no more for myself."

"Yeah, I was going to put it out and keep it for later. I mean, we weren't trying to offend you. I was actually getting ready to cover my ears, thinking you were about to scold us for using drugs or something."

"Open up the door, man. Let me out," I said to Cole, hitting the passenger-side window. It was November in Georgia, the temperature about forty degrees, and the chill in the air had me second-guessing what I had done. How did I misread my boys? How come I felt so calm about going along with something I truly didn't believe in, rather than standing and telling them off? I just put my hands on my head. I had no idea that one puff was supposed to make the body relax, be-cause it didn't do that for me. I was pissed at myself for hav-ing such low self-esteem that it seemed I'd do almost anything to fit in. Damarius and Cole came up on either side of me.

"I'm not trying to talk, y'all. Just forget the whole thing."

"Naw, man, we need to know, is this what you do up there at Tech—drinking and smoking?" Damarius asked.

"Look, I don't need the third degree about it, okay?"

"Man, you got too much on the line to be messing it up."

"Obviously, it was a one-time thing," Cole said to Damar-ius. "He got all choked up. He don't even know how to smoke it."

"Why would you do it then?" My friend asked the magic question I had been pondering.

"School has been hard. Y'all don't understand, if it ain't one thing it's another, and a big part of me is tired of always trying to uphold what is good. Maybe if I walked on the bad side of life, it wouldn't be so hard. Maybe I just didn't want any friction with y'all."

"We love friction with you, boy," he said, pushing me in the chest.

"You were always the one who was telling me to lighten up."

"But what do I know? I barely got out of high school, fool." All three of us chuckled.

"For real, I got so many friends at USC that stay in trouble, and I would be right with them if I didn't hear your voice in the back of my head whispering, 'Come on, Cole. You know that ain't right, man.' You think I want that to change? I'm the first one every weekend trying to see your highlights."

"I was actually about to get in my car," Damarius said, "and come up there and beat that teammate of yours' behind when y'all were on the field fighting. I didn't know if you needed backup, but that crap was unlike you. I don't know, dude. I know people change, but people ain't supposed to change like that. You got it together too much."

I looked at them both and then just looked away. It was the first time I had ever heard them respect me for having values, and their sincerity truly warmed me inside. However, I was stone-cold mad at myself. Why did I need the approval of others? Why did I so desperately need to fit in? Didn't I like who I was even when I was alone? Sometimes in life, there just wasn't a resolution or answers. This might just be something I was going to have to live with.

The next morning when I got home, I found a ruckus going on in my apartment. Lance and Deuce were tussling on the floor.

"What's going on, guys?"

"He's trying to drink more of the bottle, man."

"Deuce, man, naw."

"Get off me, Lance, get off me. I'm grown; I can do what the heck I want to do."

"Perry, can you do me a favor and get rid of the bottle?" Lance and I hadn't talked in a week or more. I wasn't mad anymore. I just wasn't going to talk to him until he talked to me. I guess he felt the same way, and time had just passed. But now that was over, and we had another crisis on our hands.

The last project we had worked on together was trying to get Deuce ready for his exam. Now it appeared we had more of the same. I took the vodka and poured it down the sink. Lance let Deuce up, and he came over quickly and socked me in the jaw. I was too pissed to hit him back, but I did shake him up.

"What is wrong with you? Why are you acting like this, man?"

I felt like a hypocrite asking him questions I had been asking myself, but he was taking things way over the top. I had only one puff; he was becoming a lush.

"Coach pulled me in, okay? That test I had a few weeks back? I failed it. I have to get at least a B on the final or I'm out of here. I'm trying to numb the pain. It ain't like I ever had my dad living with me, like you two. My mom worked three jobs just to take care of me and my brothers and sisters. This football thing is my chance. If I get kicked out, I'm screwed." He sank to the kitchen floor.

"I'm sorry, man, I didn't know," I said, bending down to him.

Lance came over and said, "You need to talk to us. Drinking is only ruining you."

"I don't understand what the teachers are teaching here. I should have gone somewhere else. Coach just made it seem so good that I could start as a freshman. I never thought what good that would do me if I never made it to my sophomore year. What am I going to do, y'all? I don't even want to think about it. Drinking just helps erase it, you know?"

"It's a lot, but we will get through it together."

"The dumb stuff I did get right was the stuff I remember y'all helping me with."

"Yeah, well, maybe that was a little too late. Maybe we need to start early—two or more weeks before the test."

"Hang in there with us, and let us help you get through this."

"Y'all gonna help me? Y'all don't even like each other."

"Deuce, man," Lance said, "you know you and I don't have a lot of siblings, and the ones we have don't all get along at times, but that kind of bond never breaks." He put his fist in the middle, and Deuce joined him. The two of them then looked at me, and I smiled and put my fist to theirs.

Yeah, I had issues, but who in the world didn't? And because I had people in the world who cared about me, I was going to be okay. I hoped.

The week was flying by faster than an Olympic sprinter. It was now Thursday—Thanksgiving—and I was at my grandmother's house. I couldn't contain my laughter as I heard my dad say, "Mom, you can't let both of those men come over here. That's just not cool."

"Son, I know how to handle my business. They're both my good friends, they both need their bellies filled, and I'm too old to play the field. They both know about the other one."

"So, y'all just one big happy family?" my dad said sarcastically. "Ma, you not giving it up to both of them men, are you?"

"Boy, I could come over there and smack you. Your daughter, Payton, is on her way over here. Remember who I am—the one who keeps you in check, not the other way around. Honey, I ain't feeling good. I don't have much longer on this earth, I just know it, I just know it."

"Ma, what are you talking about?" my dad said, coming closer to her.

I loved that lady so much, I hoped she was just being dramatic. I couldn't deal with this being the end. I came around the corner and said, "Grandma, you alright? What do you mean, this is the end?"

"Too much like your daddy, always listening to grown folks' conversations. What I mean is that I am an old woman too set in my own ways to be told by my son, grandson, dead husband's memories, and even the Lord Himself what I can and cannot do. Well, I take that last part back. The Lord has been telling me to enjoy my time here. And if I want to entertain my men friends, then that's my business. Now move over, my chitlings are boiling.

"Honey," my mom called out, "you need to come in here to see this. You guys better come here." She was in the living room, and when my dad and I reached her, we heard arguing in the carport.

"She invited you here? Today is my day; you know I see her on Thursdays," the old man with glasses thicker than a microscope said to the other.

"I can't keep up with the days. Shoot, I thought today was Wednesday. She just told me she was fixing some collard greens and I needed to be over here at eleven o'clock. It's eleven o'clock and I'm over here," the one barely able to stand said as he wobbled his cane.

"See, I told Momma this would be a bad idea."

I could only scratch my temple; I couldn't believe what was going on. My grandma had two dudes about to throw themselves down for her.

"What's all the fuss about?" my grandma said, coming from the kitchen. My mother, my father, and I moved to the side and allowed her to see for herself. Then she went out to the carport and set both of those men straight.

She said, "Listen here, this is my house and I cooked Thanksgiving dinner. I'm guessing that neither one of y'all brought anything but your boney selves. So get in there and sit down, and when my granddaughter gets here, we'll begin eating."

They both quickly said okay and walked in. I leaned over to my dad and said, "You've got to admit, your mom's a bad girl."

He popped me on my leg. "Shut up, son."

Payton pulled up about twenty minutes later, and to me it was right on time because Grandma had the house smelling good. The scent from the yams mixed with the scent from the yeast rolls; I didn't want nobody to get in her way.

"Who's this joker you brought here?" my dad said to Payton. I was paying more attention to each dish my grandma was putting on her table than to the door. "It's not a Bulldog, is it?"

"Dad, I'm a little dog," Payton said.

I quickly turned and said, "Tad, what's up, man?" Though I knew my sister's boyfriend well, it seemed kind of odd seeing him a couple of days before we were to play the state's biggest football rivals. I had to admit, Georgia had more wins than Tech, but they had two losses on the season and we had only one. We were going to be gunning for blood. We slapped hands.

"Aw, get them from around my table; I'm not ready yet," my grandma said.

Tad and I walked out to the carport.

"It's going to be a big game today, isn't it?" he said to me. "Man, you are jamming, and that new freshman running back y'all got—I'm glad he didn't come to Georgia. I might have lost my spot.

"That's Deuce, my roommate."

"That's how you play the game," Tad said, as I nodded with enthusiasm.

"Alright, so what's up?"

"What? What do you mean?"

"Your sister's been all worried about you, stressing me out, having me pray for you practically every day."

"Y'all prayers have been working for me, I guess. My stats look pretty good."

"Man, I'm a Bulldog. Don't get me wrong, I haven't been wanting you to do bad on the field, but that ain't what I've been praying for."

"Oh, then what?"

"Your spirit. Your soul. Mainly your walk with God."

"How is that?"

"He cares what you do on the football field as much as you care, but being a standout wide receiver ain't gonna get you no rewards in Heaven."

I had to look away; no one had ever really asked me that tough question in a while. I stayed away from my chaplain on purpose.

"A lot of temptation around you, huh?" Tad said when I didn't respond.

"True enough, Tad. I don't even know how to please God anymore."

"Well, have you opened up the Bible to see what He calls you to do?"

"If I'm not reading a playbook or a textbook, I'm asleep. When do I have time for that?"

"Bro', I ain't wit' you all the time, but I'm sure you make time for whatever it is that you want to do—see a girl, check out a club, celebrate after a game. The Lord ain't gone away, but He can only be where you allow Him to be in your life. I am not walking in your shoes, but we wear pretty much the same size. You know what I'm saying?"

"Yeah, I do."

"Payton and I barely make it. Every week, I fight on the field for yardage. It ain't Tech, but it ain't kindergarten. School kicks my butt. My momma needs money back home, and you know they don't pay us anything. The pressure is on me from every side."

"So, how do you stay so strongly rooted in your faith?"

"I learn scripture and I quote it. 'Come to me all of you that are heavy-laden and I will give you rest. Take my yoke upon you, and learn of me because my yoke is easy and light.' All I give is all my woes to him. I release them. Whatever is gonna be is gonna be. If the Lord wants it to work out, then it will. I don't want to get in the way of His big plan for me. I know I'm trying to make it sound simple, but I firmly believe that if you put Him in the midst of your madness, you can handle it."

I shook my head, and was very thankful for the conversation. I smiled even bigger when my grandma yelled, "Time to eat."

"No . . . *no!*" A bunch of us heard a teammate scream as we got dressed for the game against Georgia. Everyone immediately stopped; the sound just didn't seem rational. Next we heard banging on the trainers' walls. Looking around at my teammates' faces, I saw no one had a clue. But whatever was going on, we all knew it wasn't right.

Deuce came over to me and said, "It's Lenard."

I rolled my eyes. Whatever was going on with the chump was good for him. I mean, he was just a hothead. He thought he was the stuff, and was absolutely irritating to deal with. Coming to practice late, giving half an effort. It made no sense for a guy trying to make it to the pros to keep ticking off the coaches. Everyone knew that the scouts talked to the people who knew the players best. I sat down to strap up my cleats, but then we heard even more crying.

Deuce said, "Interstate 85 is shut down."

A couple of people turned on the different TVs in the locker room. At the bottom of the screen scrolled news of a deadly car crash. I felt like an idiot.

"I think it's his uncle," Deuce said. My heart ached as if being torn like a piece of paper into bits. I didn't want to listen to any more TV. I didn't want to speculate that what was being said by the players was true. I needed facts. No, Lenard and I weren't close, and although it made no sense at all to any of my teammates, I went to the trainers' room. I just let my soul lead. I didn't know much about Lenard, but I knew he loved his uncle and his aunt. They had raised him. If they were gone, he would need help to get through, and the only thing that I could think of that he loved as much as them was playing football. The trainers were standing with their hands up in the air. He was walking around in circles, bending some and then hitting the desk, just trying to sort it all out, I guess.

I said, "Hey, man," not even knowing that my eyes were filled with tears. And when he saw my sincerity, he fell into my arms.

"Somebody done killed my folks, man. This ain't right. This is hard. My uncle always spoke to me before every game, even when we had our issues."

"You'll have plenty time to grieve and to go over to the site. Right now, man, you know what he'd be wanting you to get ready for? I'm the X. You're the Y. We gotta play for him."

"Don't start, man. These coaches don't care about anything. They just want me to strap up. It's all about the win."

"Naw, dude, it's all about honoring him this way. Your uncle loved watching you play. He loved watching the DBs eat both our dust. He told me so. You know down deep in your heart he'd want you to play."

About thirty minutes later, Coach Red said a prayer for Lenard's aunt and uncle. We took the field as a united team, all surrounding our troubled teammate. Word must have spread through the crowd, because on Lenard's first touchdown, the crowd was on its feet. The cat that was known for cutting up in the infield just fell to his knees and bawled some more. Coach let him go ahead and take the foul. Coach talked to the ref, and the other ten players who were out there gathered around him and gave him even more of our support.

The more I stayed in my own skin, the more I knew it was hard—not the game of football, but the game of life. Situations and circumstances made you friends with your enemies. When we won the game against Georgia, which had beat us many times before, I quickly went over and hugged Lenard, and I realized that tragedies and triumphs could bring unity like nothing else ever could.

I thought Lenard was self-centered. I truly thought he was a sexist. I detested a lot of his ways. In our embrace, however, I felt that he was broken enough. As I clutched him tighter, I prayed that he would feel that he wasn't alone. Many of us often stuck around after the game to joke and watch other football games, especially when we played early, but no one did that day. Someone had lost their parents; he needed love. And though none of us knew what to say to help him through this moment, he let us know that what we were doing made a difference.

Just when we were about to head up for dinner, Coach Sanders came in and made an announcement. "Mario has been taken to the hospital."

"What?" Lenard said, forgetting his own drama. Several things immediately began swirling around in my head, none of them good. Both of us started asking Coach Sanders questions.

"Look, I don't have any answers," the coach said.

My cell phone was on vibrate and it started moving around. I couldn't believe that I was receiving a text from Mario. His butt was supposed to be in the hospital. I read: "At Emory Emergency Come ASAP." He wanted me to come to the hospital, but I knew he was dealing with criminals and I didn't feel comfortable going alone. I certainly wanted someone to know where I would be. After I explained it to Deuce, he said, "Aw, man, I'm going with you."

"Naw, I don't want to make too much of it. I just wanted to let you know where I was going, okay?"

"Alright, you got it?"

"Yeah, I got it. I need to take care of this on my own. See what he wants."

Making up some excuses about why I needed to see Mario, I finally managed to get to his cubicle. I was even able to slip past our offensive coordinator, who was already in the waiting room.

"Good to see you." I couldn't believe his arm was all bandaged up.

"I was supposed to throw the game with Georgia, but you . . . you were in my head, you know? Everything going on with Lenard was just too much for me. I couldn't do it, and they made me pay. My season is over. I just need you to keep silent, man. I'ma need a place to hide out in case they want to come back and finish what they started. You told me to do the right thing. And don't think of bailing. I need your help dealing with much."

# ~ 13 ~

# Staying the Course

"I'm there for you, man. What do you need?" I said enthusiastically, not realizing the consequences for taking in a marked man.

"I got to go to the coach's office after I get through talking to the few policemen here. I got some clothes in my locker, then I'll be ready to crash at your place."

When I didn't check in with Deuce, he called me. "You alright boy?" he said as I waited by the car for Mario.

"Yeah, I'm straight. I'm glad you're there for him, man."

"He gonna be able to play in the game? You know we're gonna be playing against Florida State?"

"Oh, so they won?" I said, getting back into football mode. If Florida State beat Boston College, they were the team we'd play in the ACC championship game down in Jacksonville. Both teams were undefeated in the conference, and even though we were as well, we didn't believe playing either team would be easy. However, if we had a choice, we felt we stood a better chance competing against Boston College. And now coming this Saturday, it looked like we were going to have to pull out all the stops to win.

"Naw, bro', his arm is broke."

"Sprained, Perry, or broke?"

"Boy, I know the difference. What did I just say?"

"Shucks, that means even if we go to a bowl game, we . . ."

"Put the letters BCS in front of Bowl Game because we're going to the best bowls out there."

As soon as Mario and I pulled out of the hospital parking lot, I had second thoughts. He started ordering me to do this and that, to drive this way and that way, to pull into the gas station and get him a soda. But I tried to keep my calm knowing that maybe the Lord was trying to do something with me, such as humble me to serve. I believed the stand Mario had taken to get himself back on track was the correct one. Now he just needed help to maintain it. But after I dropped him off in front of the football facility door, I became paranoid when he called and said, "Don't just sit there and wait for me. Somebody could have been watching you when you dropped me off. If I'm going to be at your crib, nobody should know."

"Well, what type of car am I supposed to be looking for?" I asked.

"That's just it. Those guys drive all types of cars. They do this kind of stuff all the time. I'ma be upstairs with Coach for a minute, and if you go to the other side of the stadium, I'll have one of the trainers bring me out that way. Just make sure no one follows you."

Okay, now this was serious, 'cause it wasn't just me having to look out for Mario. I had two roommates, and I hadn't cleared this with them, and when Mario was back in the car, all I could think about was them.

When I was silent, he finally asked, "Man, you alright? I got you I'ma make sure don't nobody hurt you."

"Boy, you got a broke arm," I half-teased, almost serious. How could he look out for me? If he was that big and bad, how come he needed to stay with me in the first place? This was going to be a lot, but there was no turning back. As soon as we got to my place and we shut the door, Lance bit no tongue and said, "What's he doing here with a bag? For real, Perry, he's not staying here." He said it so loud that Deuce came out of his room.

"Hey, man, Mario, what's up? I'm glad you're okay," Deuce said to him, helping him sit down on the couch.

"Naw, I'm serious, Deuce. He don't need to get comfortable," Lance said, bending down to get his bag. Deuce snatched it out of his hand.

"Come on, come on y'all," I said, pointing toward my bedroom door.

"I ain't trying to cause no problems, but y'all just work that out," Mario said.

"Perry, we live here, too, man. How could you just go and invite him here? You know what he's into. You know how I feel about it. We've fallen out before about it, and now you gonna bring him into our home?"

"We all know what he's into. My suspicions from the beginning were completely right. He's mixed with the wrong people. He's gambling on our games. They wanted him to throw the Georgia game, and he wouldn't. They just tore his butt up at a gas station, threatening to come and do more. What am I to do? Leave him out there? We've got an extra room."

"You're not giving him Collin's room. If anything, he's going to sleep in yours and you're going to sleep on the couch," Lance said to me, getting in my face. Deuce jumped in between us and said, "Alright, you two, back down. You ain't the only one who lives here. I'm sure it's only temporary. Why does anybody gotta sleep on the couch? That's stupid. We have a room. Didn't you hear what he said? The man stood for something finally. We beat Georgia. I'm sure if he was supposed to throw it, somebody lost a heck of a lot of money."

The three of us were silent for a second; everybody was contemplating this whole ordeal on their own. I'm sure it was a ton of mixed emotions. Even a part of me was glad that Mario was feeling the wrath of his ways. But if folks were crazy enough and upset enough to take him down during broad daylight over some loot, it was certainly not over yet.

"But we can't keep him safe; we can't keep this from Coach. Certainly, Perry, you're agreeing now that we have to tell somebody?"

"I don't know. I just know that right now, he needs to recuperate and he needs to rest. He came through for us. Can we come through for him?"

"And more so than that," Deuce said, "Lenard ain't going to be able to play. You gonna be starting, Lance. He wouldn't be the one you would want to be pissing off right now. You need him on your side."

"He doesn't need to teach me anything."

"Whatever then."

We heard a tap on my door, and Deuce opened it up. Mario stood in the doorway looking seriously pitiful.

"Hey, man, I spoke too soon concerning you staying here. It's not my place alone."

"And if you leave, know it ain't me," Deuce said, throwing his hands up in the air.

"Alright, Lance," Mario began, "I know I've said some foul stuff to you practically all season. I was just trying to mess with your head. You got some skills that I'm just a little envious of. But right now, as tough of a façade as I put up, I'm embedded with some bad people."

"I know. They beat me up, remember?" Lance said, reminding me again of how dangerous this whole situation was.

"I don't think they'll come back here. They know you and I ain't on the same page and would never think you would give me shelter. I don't deserve it, but I need y'all to let me stay."

"Fine, whatever," Lance said, heading out of my room.

Hopefully, it was the right move, because now that he was here, we were all in it.

The next morning, I woke up excited that all was well. The windows were intact, the door wasn't broken down, and the four people that slept in the house were still alive and kicking.

It was going to be such a big week. It still hadn't sunk in to me that we were about to play the ACC championship game. In the flash of an eye, I recalled the first game of the season. I don't know whether it was nerves or I just needed to get the game tighter, but I never thought I'd manage to turn it around so well, especially considering the rollercoaster ride my personal life seemed to be on. It was major that my academics and athletics were both on point.

Thinking that my houseguest needed to be fed, I decided to whip up some eggs and bacon. But when I cracked the door, I was really surprised to see Lance and Mario sitting on the couch in a deep discussion—so deep that they didn't even notice me standing in my doorway. So naturally, I listened.

"I just hate that the papers are saying that I'm not going to be able to do it, that we're for sure going to lose now. Maybe they're right. I wanted this opportunity so bad, and now I'm the main one wishing that your arm wasn't broke. What kind of leader am I going to be on Saturday?"

"The one who's going to stop feeling sorry for himself, the one who knows he's capable. I never doubted that you could do it, Lance. Your arm has more distance than mine. It just seems like you get hit a little bit in practice and you wimp up. Florida State has some big boys, and they're going to be ready to skin your tail alive. No telling how the fickle Tech fans will support you. Florida State is going to have a crowd, and no matter what happens, you must maintain your composure. If we fall behind, you can't get frustrated. If we pull ahead, you can't get a big head. If we tie, you've got to believe you can pull it out. I don't know if I'm even going to travel to the game, so I'm going to say this now: Tell yourself you can, and you will."

Lance looked over at Mario and nodded. I couldn't believe the two of them were able to coexist under the same roof, much less care deeply enough to encourage one another. I was moved. But when they noticed me, it was awkward and I teased, "Do I need to go get some tissue or something?"

"No, I just need to admit that I was wrong," Lance said, "and you were right."

"Well, I know that," I said, messing with them both, "but what am I right about this time?"

"That this guy here ain't that bad. But I still think you need to go to the police," Lance said, looking at Mario. Mario got up off the couch and said, "You need to stay out of that. You know they're crazy."

"Yeah, but we can't hide you here forever."

"Yeah, I know. I was thinking about that last night. I'm not going to put this on y'all. I'm going to go talk to them."

"What do you mean, you're going to go talk to them?" I said, sounding concerned.

Lance said, "Look, we're not just going to let you put yourself in danger like that."

It was actually weird. Just yesterday, he didn't even want Mario in the house. Now the two of them were "over the top" friends. It was cool, and I agreed with Lance, so I said, "He's right. You ain't leaving."

"Let me say this so y'all understand. You guys are the rookies, the freshmen; I run things around here, even with my broke arm. I'm leaving. I've already run away from a lot of things. I finally stood up to them and refused to throw the dag on the Georgia game. Now I've got to finish what I started. I just needed to get my head clear, and it's clear now. I can't run, and I can't get y'all involved. If y'all care so much, y'all can feed a brother."

I laughed, remembering that was what I was on my way to do. Although I had no idea what Mario was planning to do or say to the crew he had the beef with, I knew it wasn't for me to stop him, and I really respected that he rethought dragging us into it all. Deuce had been fast asleep, but when he smelled my bacon, he got up to grab himself a piece just before it was all gone.

A phone rang, and all four of us looked at our cells. "It's me. It's me," I said, messing with them, until I looked at the number and realized it was Coach Sanders. *What now?* was all I could think. He never dialed me up unless it was urgent.

"What's up, Coach? I'm supposed to see you in a minute for a team meeting. Everything alright?"

With his good hand, Mario waved me off. "It ain't important; it's just coach, checking in on his player," I said to him. I waved back, getting caught up in his liveliness.

Coach Sanders got me refocused when he said, "I need you back in my office now, Perry."

"Every—"

"Just get here."

Twenty minutes later, I saw Coach Sanders pacing in front of his office door.

"What took you so long, man?" he said.

"I had to get dressed, Coach."

"Alright, alright."

"What's going on?"

"It's Lenard. He hasn't left my office all night. I went with him to the morgue. The chaplin talked to him. We thought he was okay. I'm not insensitive to what he's going through, but he just broke down on me again, and I remembered you got through to him yesterday. I'm not into huggy-feely kind of stuff. I'm a football coach; it's about Xs and Os with me. But I know this is a new wound and it's got to heal, so just get in there and talk to him."

He opened the door, and closed it just as fast as soon as I was on the other side. As hard as it slammed, I was amazed that Lenard never even looked up to see what the commotion was. He was in a trance, sitting like a zombie, staring into space. What was I to say? I just prayed silently: *Lord, I don't know what to say to this guy. You're going to have to speak for me. I mean, he has nobody now. These people raised him. They died on their way to watch him play. I mean, it's just a lot. At least I have Payton. As tough as Lenard has led me to believe he is, he is now completely broken.*

I said Lenard's name three times, and when he didn't respond, I shook him. "Lenard, what's wrong man?"

And then, like a light switch turning on, he went off, using all kinds of words I didn't understand and ordering me to get out.

I was confused. I didn't know. Should I leave him? Should I stay? The words slipped from my tongue angrily: "God, didn't You hear me ask You what to do?" I hit my head hard on the back of the door and slid down, wishing I had answers.

"You prayed for me?" Lenard asked.

Without even looking at him, I just nodded my head. Yeah, I prayed for him, but I was disgusted, at my wit's end. But God was about to show me, because little did I know that had moved him. He sat down beside me and just opened up.

"That man tucked me into bed every night, in some form

or other, ever since I was five. He either physically did it, called me on the phone, left me a text message, or simply told me to remember he was praying for me. They couldn't have any children of their own—something about his wife's ovaries. My mom was messing around with stuff. Heck, I was a crack baby, truth be known. But they worked with me through all of that. I know I still have issues, and I just don't know how I'm going to make it without them. All the coaches do is think about football. Who's going to help me bury my folks, man?"

"We're all here to help you do that."

"My uncle worked for MARTA, Perry. We ain't rich. And with him not dying on the job, I don't know what the insurance will cover. I talked to a couple of burial services, and I don't have enough money to bury them. How am I supposed to think about football when I can't give my folks a proper good-bye? I can't look ahead feeling guilty about the past, you understand?"

We sat quietly for a moment. Lenard was contemplating there not being any hope, and I was desperately trying to think of a way to bump into a truckload of it. Out of the blue, he said, "I could cremate them, I guess. They told me that was the cheapest option. I ain't one for cemeteries, but I feel I need somewhere to visit them. I just really don't want to go that route. I'm all messed up, Perry, trying to figure this thing out."

"You've got to get out of here. Lenard, you've got to get some rest."

"I tried closing my eyes, but all I could think of was the two of them in a cold icebox, unable to move, turn, or get up. And my throat felt like it was caving in; my heart started beating harder than from anything I have ever experienced on a football field. It just is too much right now. I can't think."

Really needing God's help on this one, I stood up, reached out my hand, and said, "Let me help you up?"

"You're not hearing me, Perry. I want to be down. I don't want to feel good. I don't want to play in no game. I just want to be left alone. But you got to understand, Perry, well . . . What happens when you die, Perry? I can't believe I'm asking you anything, but do you know?"

"Well, obviously, I'm not dead, but I know four things."

"Alright, what?"

"First you got to get up." I extended my hand again and pulled him up. "The Bible says that to be absent of the body is to be present with the Lord, and it says that the Lord is going to provide us with a place that no man can imagine. Your uncle told me he liked me because I was a Christian. He was a believer and he felt that I was on the right track. If God's word says that when you are not here, you are with Him, and it's supposed to be a place that is wonderful for those who believe, and your uncle believed, then the last thing you got to know and trust is that he's okay, whether you bury him or cremate him. He's with God."

Water fell from Lenard's eyes as if he was sweating. "I'm tired."

"Come on, go get some rest." We opened the coach's door and he was off. Of course, Coach Sanders cornered me and made me give him a recap of our hour-long conversation.

"I know the coaches will help him to bury them," I said.

"Yeah, we'll get that handled. Ain't no need to stress over that."

I got the okay to head up and get some lunch before the meetings. I picked up my cell and automatically called my own father. It's amazing how someone else going through something makes you reflect what you are going through and appreciate your situation.

"I want to help him, Dad, but I don't know what to do. I'm just me. Well, I grew up down there and . . ."

So you still haven't gotten it, huh?"

"What do you mean, Dad?" I said into the cell while walking toward the café.

"Everybody's familiar with you and Lenard as athletes, for your individual talents as well as for your little tiffs on the green. I always thought Tech fans could do more, support more, be present more, but your mom is right—those are some loyal people. You're interviewed about the game all of the time, and that's important. But maybe the next time you get in front of the camera, you can stand for something even bigger."

I got it. Truly finishing something you started went way beyond making an apology or telling somebody you were going to do something without ever doing it or responding with actions. Lenard needed my help. I went straight to the Athletics Director and told her that I had a statement:

*A lot of people are asking me if I am excited about going to the ACC game. Quite honestly, I am a little bit distracted. As many of you know, a teammate that I have had personal issues with has lost two people dear to him. And as everybody knows, NCAA players do not collect a paycheck for what we do. I'm not trying to be politically correct here. We need our fans to help. If you have anything—a dime, a dollar, twenty dollars—to help with the fees associated with the burial, please send it in to the athletic department in his name. Our fans demand a lot from us players, and rightly so, being that this is your school, but right now we need you. Thanks, Perry Skky Jr."*

"Wow," the AD said after taping my statement. "That was moving." She said she had to first run it by Coach Red, but then she'd send it over to our radio network.

"I don't know if it'll help," I said.

"I'm sure it will. We have great people at our school."

I walked out of there and didn't need any lunch. I felt full; I felt good. I felt like God was using me. For so long, I had been really uneasy about trying to find my way. Now, I had put myself out there and was trying to be a part of something. Who knew how it would turn out. I found I cared more about informing than about my own reputation. Somehow it was going to work out. God was going to bless me; I was staying the course.

# ~ 14 ~

# Inspiring My Soul

"Perry, this last week has been the hardest week of my life," Lenard said to me as we road the bus to our hotel in Jacksonville. "Thanks to you, I've been able to get through it."

I grinned; I was humbled. I went through the majority of the season despising him for being arrogant and shallow. I'd wished so many bad things on him. Watching him during the funeral a few days before, I felt a little guilty. Although it was hard for him, he was a true man, I realized. He moved me in ways I didn't even know I could be moved in.

"You getting all those Tech people to send in money, I just don't know how I would have made it without you, is all I'm trying to say. And I am ready now to play some football."

"Well, alright then," I said, wanting to lighten the mood. Then he hit me hard in the arm.

"Ouch!"

"I just want to know, can yo' boy Lance handle it? I got some boys from Florida State, and they can't wait to mess him up."

"I know, I know. He's gonna surprise them, though. They think he's gonna play like a player with no experience. He won a state championship last year, and although it was high school, I have never seen him crack under pressure."

"Yeah, I watched a little bit of his film. I just don't know if I should say something to him, if that'll help or throw him off, ya know? I want to get him pumped up, but he's supposed to be the leader of the team now—I need him to come to me."

"With everything you have helped us all overcome, we are more than ready for Florida State."

Because the game would be early the next day, we had chapel that night. I felt a little guilty because I had stayed away from our chaplin, even though I knew he wasn't the kind of man who would force us to pursue our walk with God. However, there were so many other things that kept coming up, that kept me away from concentrating on my priority. I knew I needed to sit in the first row, to take in every word he said.

"Wow! It's good to see you here," he said. The two of us were alone in the meeting room.

"After the game next week, you got some time?" I asked him.

"My office is always open, man. Come on by."

"Cool."

Once the room was full, he began. "Men, confidence is the key. You can do it, you can win this game, but only if you know that what is in you is more than enough to help you become victorious." I looked over at Lance, who was sitting beside me, and although he was tuned in as if the talk was specifically for him, I knew he had his own issues. But the talk was for me too. "The text for today is Daniel, chapter six."

I was familiar with the story of Daniel. I couldn't wait to see what spin was about to be put on this old testament story. I knew that when C. Morris was fired up, it was going to be good.

He continued, "Daniel had favor on his life. Even when a

bunch of haters joined together to make Daniel lose favor with the king, he kept rising to the top. Such is the case with you all and the whole ACC conference. With each week, more and more teams have been gunning for you. You've withstood, though. Now, you're standing at the finale, just one game to go. They're creating distractions with things that have made us stronger. These things are *not* our weaknesses. Oh, but they don't know who we are, they're trying to manipulate the game. They're trying to throw us in the lion's den, thinking we're going to get torn apart. Trying to make us believe that what we say doesn't hold water. However, just like Daniel got thrown in the lion's den because he loved the Lord, he believed God would see him through. Those that tried to slay him were slain themselves."

C. Morris threw his clipboard, then kicked a chair. He stood on the desk and stomped.

"I'm mad y'all. Folks are saying our defense has never been tested, that our special team is horrible because our kicker won't bounce back from his ankle sprain. Our wide receivers will be distracted because of the tragedy and our new quarterback has no poise. Anybody believe the hype?"

Lots of us shouted, "NO!"

"Anybody believe the hype?" he asked more forcefully, jumping down from the desk and getting in our faces.

More of us roared out, "NO!"

"Then believe in you, you as not just the offense, you as not just the defense, you as not just special teams, but you as the whole Georgia Tech football team. Now go out there and win."

Next, Coach Red addressed us. "Wow, that was moving. Man, I took something from that talk. The report out there is that we can't. Let's show them that we can. Anybody with me?" We all jumped to our feet. "Well, get a good night's rest, and see you in the morning."

I woke up early the next day. The sun didn't even beat me. And I fell to my knees and said: "Lord, I have let You down so much, but You're showing more and more what life is all about. It's not always going to be touchdown city. There will be an interception or two for me every now and then. But You're showing me how to stay in the game, how to find the good in people. I want to win today, and I want You to get the glory for it, but if we don't win, Lord, I want You to get the glory, too."

It was game time, and on the opening play, although we thought we were ready, we kicked it to them and their man ran it back for a touchdown. Instantly, just like that, without warning, we were behind. They kicked it to us, and Lenard caught the ball but let it drop through his hands. Their men came running down fast, and he recovered, but we had to start at the five. Lance's turn was up. On the first offensive play, the coaches put the game in Deuce's hands. He was stopped for a two-yard loss. Now we were on the three. The next two plays were passes, and both were batted down. The whole first half went that way, and when we went in for halftime, we were down by 21. We scored not one point, and Coach Red let us have it.

"I don't know if y'all remember the talk from last night, but I feel like y'all are in the lion's den. They're coming your way, and they're trying to eat you alive, but you've got to believe that you're not going to be harmed and that you're going to come through untouched. Reverse this thing. Throw them in there; make sure they're eaten. Can we do it, men? Can we win? I know you can, but you have to believe it."

Thirty minutes later we did! Standing in the middle of the field with my teammates getting the ACC trophy made me completely realize that if you believed, and gave your whole heart, and trusted that God knew what was best, He could deliver you, and for us that day he did.

"What, Perry, you thought I was going to chase you down?" the chaplain said to me as I sat in his office for my counseling session.

"Naw, not chase me down, but—I don't know—call me and ask me to come in or something."

"Naw, buddy, this is your salvation. I love you and I care about you, but you have to make sure you are in right with God. You've got other things that take priority, then you have to talk that out with him. If things get out of whack and you wish your life was more together and less crazy and you ain't been on your knees praying, then you haven't been spending time in the word, you haven't been attending anybody's church. Why do you think God should show up?"

He leaned back in his chair and waited for me to respond, but I agreed with him. I wanted God to be there, I wanted less turmoil, I needed to start acting more like a Christian and stop just being one.

"You know, Perry, I've watched you this year, and honestly, I don't think you should be so hard on yourself. I think you have made a valiant effort at letting folks know what you stand for. I've seen some of your interviews, and you've given God his glory. I've watched you with some of your teammates, and you've strengthened some of your weakest relationships. Only a man humbled by God could do such a thing, so you're growing."

"I guess it just doesn't seem like I'm growing at that fast a pace, I can see my results on the football field. You know all the catches and the touchdowns. I even see results in the classroom. Though I have to study more than I did in high school, I'm finding it is paying off. I just don't see it in my

Christian walk. Can we talk, can we really talk?" I asked him, "People think I have it all together, but I am struggling with so much."

"Yeah, I hope you always know this is a confidential session, and I ain't doing no judging. What's up? What's going on with ya?"

"People just place so much on me. Like I'm supposed to always be good—good at sports, good at academics, good at feeling good about myself. And I guess maybe as hard as I try to keep up the image in the first few areas, I truly struggle with the self-esteem thing—wanting to be better, and thinking I don't measure up enough."

"But to whose standard, Perry?" he asked, as if the imaginary bar I was trying to be held up to was really being held by no one.

"I'ma tell you, son, you are a good athlete, and a pretty smart joker, too. I don't think I could have gotten into Georgia Tech. I'm just going to be honest about it, but by the grace of God, I am here for His purpose, not education, so it really doesn't matter. But my point in all of that is, as good as you are, you're still nothing without Christ within you. Because we have some players on this team who are barely passing, if you ever run into a class that you can't keep up in, they'll get rid of your tail. Stop training and stop working hard or get hurt—career over! But what's in your heart, who you accepted to be the Lord of your life, can never be taken from you. Actually, you haven't even received the greatest reward from all he wants to give you. I'm not saying to build on the success you have in this world. Make no mistake, the most you need to give is this heavenly praise."

I quickly nodded. I heard every word he said, and I understood.

"You're not trying to stir up treasures on earth, man. You're not someone because of who you are. Your self-esteem, your self-worth is awesome, on point, all that, the bomb, the best, because the person who is the king of kings, the lord of lords, the Almighty, the beginning and the end, lives inside of you."

"Yeah!" I said, understanding it more and more as he talked. I could wake up in the morning and feel like I gained a few extra pounds. I might not like it, but God still loved me. I could play in the bowl game and not catch anything, but God still loved me. I could bomb my final exams. My parents would be pissed, but God would still love me.

"You've got to learn to love yourself, Perry," he continued, "as God loves you. Unconditionally. Yeah, there's nothing wrong with bettering yourself and working on your weaknesses, but as the song goes, if He takes care of the sparrow, you know He's got you. Work on building that, strengthening that, make that better. Don't give up on Him, because He's not giving up on you. To whom much is given much is required. You're a leader on this team not just because of your ability, but because of your influence, and I'm proud of you. Lenard came in here to talk to me. The knucklehead joker had been so against God for so long, but because of you and your walk, he's praised and received Christ in dealing with his own personal loss. God is using you, Perry."

Silently I thought: *Use me more, Lord. You helped me to know it's cooler to do things for You than it is to do things for me.*

"We've got the off-season coming up, and we can get together then and really have some disciple sessions."

I asked, "Why do I have to wait?"

"Boy, please. I hear y'all might have a chance at the national championship."

"Naw, we're just ranked number three. Michigan and USC, they're gonna be in the big dance."

"I don't think so. Michigan has to play Ohio State, and I really believe they can lose it."

"Yeah, but then they'd have only one loss, just like us."

"Yeah, but everybody wants to see a rematch. What you don't read in the papers is that they like you one minute and don't like you the next. I try not to listen, but everybody's hyped on you. You know it, Perry, everybody's behind this team—one player wanting to commit suicide, another player losing his guardians, quarterback being beaten up in some random attack, so they think. You guys are the Cinderella team. New coach, too. If Michigan loses, I think y'all are in that big game."

"But I think you just put it in perspective for me, though."

"Tell me, what did you get?"

"I've got to quit devaluing myself, and if I stay on my knees, God can keep reminding me that I've got all I need."

"Doesn't it feel good to know that you can't lose that position?"

For the first time in a long time, I felt connected to God. It was just like eating a pot of my grandmother's collard greens. I felt full.

With all the hard training the Tech football team did, I didn't spend time with the basketball players. I didn't even know a lot of those guys yet. And although the teams used the same facilities, we rarely were here at the same time, so I was taken completely aback when I saw the cafeteria filled to capacity. Looking around for a place to sit, I was stopped dead in my tracks when I saw Savoy smiling from ear to ear, talking with this tall, lean joker who looked like he wanted to put her on his plate and sop her up. What was that about? Was this something that happened every day. Did the two of them engage over dinner, or was this just one of those times that we all were in here and he was flirting and she was flattered. I hadn't been on my game trying to court her because every time the two of us were together, it got a little sticky. Both of us would become hotter than a steamy August afternoon. She hadn't been pursuing me, and I just assumed that she was working on her studies. Had I misjudged her distance? Had she turned her attention to another? Then my ego thought, you know what? Forget her. If that's what she wants to do, whatever.

Acting as if I didn't see them, I strolled over to get a plate. I didn't even notice what I put on my plate or how much. When I was done, it looked like I was going to eat for four offensive linemen. Thankfully, some folks had finished by the time I was ready to sit down, so I just went and sat by myself. I couldn't believe that she was still engaged with that chump.

Lenard sat down beside me and patted me on the back really hard. "Aw, cheer up, boy. It'll be alright."

"Man, what you talking about? I'm just eating."

"No, you're whining over here worse than Coach Sanders' three-year-old little boy does when his mom won't let him stay at practice."

"Oh, see, now you got jokes."

"Man, I know you see your girl Savoy is hot. That's why I wanted to get with her. That's why we've still got beef about that situation, too, leaving her out on the road."

"Man, I ain't trying to talk about that."

"Oh, so you do care? That crap I tried wasn't cool, but you know, every brother's trying."

"Well, man, we ain't dating. She can date you, she can date him, she can do whatever."

"I forgot what she told me because all she kept talking about was you, you, you, you. As if I cared about that junk. Girls just do that junk to get our attention sometimes. She noticed you when you first walked in. From what I understand, he's been telling everybody that he wants to get with her."

"Who is he?"

"Allen Lemmons."

"Oh, so that's Allen Lemmons."

"Yeah, your equivalent in basketball, boy. I can't believe you were so in your own world that you didn't pay attention to him. I don't know if she saw you or what, but that's when she got all interested in him. She's a good girl—too good for me, honestly—but man, I know this game. Most girls only want you when you're doing well, thinking you're going to have big dollars in your pocket eventually. She seems to really care about you, however. If I were you, I wouldn't let that go."

I heard what he said, and boy, did he make sense. I knew deep down I'd rather have Savoy in my life and pray all the time to stay on the straight and narrow instead of not having her in my life at all. I was barely able to breathe as I watched her laugh with another guy. I was motivated, and I knew that somehow, some way, I needed to get her back. So I thought: *Lord, did I mess up? I asked You so many times to give me a chance with Savoy, and so many times You put us back together, but have I lost her for good or was Lenard right? Was she just flirting, trying to make me jealous? If so, it worked?*

"Alright, partner, do what you gotta do. I hope Michigan or USC loses so we can get a chance. I'm ready to show the world the duo wide receiver team out there in college football. You with me? You with me? We gonna do this?" he said more hyper than I had seen him in a long time.

"Yeah, boy, we gonna do this."

I started eating my food again when trouble came my way. Charlie stood in front of me and said,

"This seat taken?" Before I had a chance to even say anything, she just sat down right in front of me. I wasn't up for playing the same game. I didn't want to talk to her, and she needed to know that up front. But before I could say anything to her, she extended her hand and started touching my face. Out of the corner of my eye, I saw Savoy looking over.

She had been in her own world the whole time, but now that she maybe felt threatened, if she wanted me at all, she turned her eyes my way.

"Come on girl, I'm eating," I said.

"I was just trying to wipe the macaroni and cheese from your chin."

"I'm a big boy. I'm fine."

"Oh, I know that," she said, flirting in the worst way.

When I looked over at Savoy, she was standing up, and she didn't look happy. Allen was getting up, too, and that didn't make me happy. Some guys just want to be out there, enjoying three or four ladies, keeping their options open, but this was a moment of decision for me. I could continue making her think we were through, or I could truly show my heart.

Then Charlie snapped and said, "I'm trying to talk to you. I've given you several opportunities to get with this," she said, pointing to her body.

I leaned in and said, "I don't know how many ways I can say to you that I am not interested. Alright? Dang." I stood up, picking up my tray and still trying to figure how I was going to handle Savoy.

I just wasn't ready when I saw Allen take his hand and put it on her waist, rub it around a little bit, and touch a few other areas. I wanted to hurt the brother so bad, it was clear what was in my heart. But that was her battle to fight, unless she found it acceptable for the guy's hands to go anywhere. The room went silent when she turned around and slapped him, then dashed out. As chatter began to fill the café again, I realized my query had been answered—we were on the same page. I cared about that girl in the worst way. Everything about her was inspiring my soul.

# Learning Our Fate

"Oh, so you just gonna stand there and not go get her?" Saxon said from behind me.

This wasn't an easy decision. Though I cared so much for the girl, she and I had simply been going through it for so long. Would we ever get it right? Were we too young for a serious relationship? Would I do her more harm than good? But when the Allen guy started going off telling everybody what he was going to do to her, he couldn't believe she hit him. I had to make sure she was okay, and deep down, the only way I knew that I could was if we were together.

"So he thinks he's going to just hit on my sister?" Saxon said, stepping in front of me.

I put my hand on his sweater and tugged him back. "I got this."

"Well, tell the brother something. You just all still and everything. Handle it."

When Allen left the cafeteria, I jetted off right behind him, not ever thinking we would have an audience as I rounded the corner. I heard tons of students exiting the café looking for some action. I didn't have time to deal with that, 'cause for real, I had to make sure there was no action to witness. I understand that he thought it wasn't cool to get a whack in public.

"Where'd she go, man?" he asked, abruptly walking in front of me.

"You need to calm down."

"Perry Skky Jr. They say you're as good in football as I am in basketball. I watched a couple of your games. Please, you weak."

"Y'all have already played eight games, and you have won only one. I already had thirteen touchdowns by now."

"Y'all don't have a perfect season either. Everybody knows Michigan and USC are going to be in the big dance. I'm just saying, if you were bad, you would have more of an effect on getting your team to win."

"Handle your team and your games before you come talking to me."

He tried to go to the left of me, but I stepped over so he couldn't. Then he tried to go the other way, and I blocked that path as well.

"Man, get out of my way."

"Where do you think you're going, all huffed up like you're going to hurt somebody?"

"You saw what that girl did, disrespecting me and everything. I don't put up with that crap. I don't let a woman think she can front me like that."

"Like everybody didn't see what you had did to her."

"She was flirting. She wanted me to do more than touch her butt. She wanted it, and now she will see that she should never have messed with me. What's it to you anyway?"

If I learned anything this semester, it was that I had several wars going on inside that I hadn't learned how to tap into. What was it to me? It was love. "That's my girl, man."

"What? She told me she didn't have anybody. I can't believe that."

"We dated in high school, now we're in college. The road's a little bumpy. What else can I say?"

"So, you struck out then. She left your tail. Now you see her with me, and you want to try to take her back. Man, please, obviously you couldn't handle your thing. I'm about to get her in line."

I put my hand on his chest.

"I know us meeting like this isn't exactly cool, but she's my girl and I need you to back off. I owe you one on this," I said, putting my hand out, hoping that he would accept.

"Alright, whatever, man," he said, hitting it lightly before turning around and telling everybody behind him to go on and mind their own business. I had no idea where to look first to find Savoy. When I went out to the parking lot, I saw her leaning over my car, apparently crying.

"Savoy?" I called out. She lifted up off of the car and ran into my arms.

"Why couldn't we make it? Why can't I get you out of my head? I know you don't care about me. I know you got with Charlie. I know . . ."

"Wait a minute," I said, cutting her off. "Before we talk about how I feel about you, where did you get this idea that I slept with Charlie? I know you saw us in the cafeteria, but it wasn't what you thought you saw."

"It was what I just saw. She told me, so you can't deny it."

"She told you what?" I had enough on my conscience for her to be mad at me for—the strip club, looking at porn, seducing her in my mind over and over again. But I flat-out told Charlie she wasn't the one months back. I was not about to own up to some reputation I didn't even want.

"You can't believe everything somebody says," I said to her as I cupped her chin in my hand and I stroked her softly. We held each other's gaze; I wanted her to know that I was telling the truth. I really felt like she knew me deep within.

"I'm not perfect, Savoy. I've got a lot of flaws. Yeah, she came over that time when I was sick and she threw herself at me. Yeah, a brother looked, but I ain't done nothing."

She cracked a little smile. "So you didn't?"

"No, no, I didn't."

"What about just a minute ago?"

"Obviously again, she must have been putting on a show for you. Y'all women have that catfight stuff going on, and I don't even understand. But forget about me. What were you doing with Allen? Giving him signals that made him think you wanted something physical?"

"Stupid," she replied. "Just trying to make you jealous. Even when I thought you had gotten with Charlie, I still wanted you. I hate myself. It's like, I will accept anything from you. And then this other part of me is like, forget him all together."

My lips met hers. Nothing was forced; it was all just natural. It was like everything she was saying I felt was true, because she kissed me back with such intensity.

"What are we going to do?" she said once we were done enjoying each other.

"It's clear that neither one of us wants to be apart. You were just trying to make me jealous when you were talking to that basketball player."

"I didn't mean to actually slap him. Yes, I did," she admitted. "I'm sure I'll have more drama from the fallout."

"Naw, I talked to him."

"You did?"

"I told him you were my girl."

"You did?"

"I asked him to leave you alone."

Before she could say anything else, I had to kiss her once again. Then I just held her tightly and verbally prayed: *Lord, this girl right here has got my heart, and I used to think this girl right here could get me into a lot of trouble. But it's pretty clear that You have shown me that that wasn't working either. Instead of us just trusting each other, help us to trust You. If we focus on being brother and sister of Christ, and boyfriend and girlfriend, or whatever else it's supposed to be called, this thing can work as long as it is supposed to for as long as You want it to. Thanks for putting us back as one.*

Folks from the café were filing out to the parking lot. We were just holding each other. The girls were cheering as some of the guys started barking. It was corny, but it felt right.

Our grades were in. I had three As and a B. Lance had all Bs. We were waiting on Deuce to come out of his room to give us a report. Lance didn't want to say he thought he's gone, nor did I want to utter negative thoughts. Taking a deep breath, I prayed: *Lord, please work it out for Deuce. This school ain't no joke. Lord, he's trying, and he is a good guy who loves You. I know you got him if this just doesn't work out, but I'm just asking.*

Then I heard his door open.

"Alright, man, just tell us."

"I just got off the phone with coach and . . ."

"And?" I replied.

"And it's good news and bad news."

"What do you mean?" Lance asked him.

I was looking at his face, trying to read him either way, but I couldn't tell. I just hoped the bad news wasn't too bad.

"I failed that class."

"Well, obviously that's the bad news," Lance said.

"Well, I got two Ds and a C."

"Dang, boy, that ain't no two point five," Lance said. "Is that the good news?" Lance asked, rolling his eyes up to the sky to say that if it was, then that's some crap.

"Naw, the good news is that I am not kicked out of here, man. I'm on academic probation. I get a chance to pull it all up. Maybe if I study all semester like I did last month, I can make it here. I have realized that it ain't all about football. I can do it."

"That's right, man, you can."

"With good friends like y'all, I'm learning that I can."

None of us was expecting the door to open, but when a key turned in the lock, we all knew who it was. It had been a long time since we had seen our sweet ol' Collin. What was going on? Was he back for good? I hoped so. As Deuce just said, we all needed a second chance sometime. Be better, feel better, and get it all straight.

"Hey, man," Lance said, going over to him.

"Hey, guys," Collin responded in a dry tone.

"Man, you ain't called us," Deuce said to him. He just shrugged his shoulders. None of us could really say anything because we hadn't reached out to him either.

"I mean, I've got to live my life for myself. Everybody's only looking out for themselves anyway."

"It ain't like that." I stepped in between Deuce, Lance, and Collin and said, "We all care."

"We might not know how to show it, being that we're all going through our own personal hells," Lance said.

"You guys don't owe me any explanation. I just came to get a few of my things."

"Oh, so you don't want to live with us anymore because we didn't call you? Man, you a dude; you not some girl we got to chase after. Didn't you just hear Perry when he said we cared?" Deuce said, getting a little angry.

"Calm down," I said.

"It's not that. I'm just going to take off for a while. Find out what I need to do next for me. Remember, I didn't even want to be here. Since that wasn't successful, I have to find out what I want to do. Plus my scholarship is gone."

"They took your scholarship?" Deuce said.

"That's not right," Lance replied.

"I mean, I'll be able to go to school here," Collin clarified. "My education is still here. But regarding my position on the field, Coach couldn't guarantee me anything. And even if he said I could play, I don't know if I'm ready to. I missed you guys. My parents told me how worried you guys were when I was out of it and stuff. Honestly, I have never had friends who cared like you guys. Deuce, you're right, I'm not a girl. I can't always want more from people. I have to be satisfied with what I get. I am realizing that I do have a few bad problems, but if I put more focus on it, maybe I could get along."

"That's right, man," I said to him.

"Man, you can come up here and hang out with us anytime. Yeah, I'm trying to get these jokers to get their groove on."

We all laughed. We'd miss him tremendously, but sometimes you had to take a few steps backward to get a good running start to push you forward. Collin was a good guy. I really felt he needed God, but I also felt he had a good heart. Once he was okay, he would make it. Lance helped him pack up.

I was in my room when Lance knocked on my door. "Hey, man, you got that magazine I let you borrow a long time ago? I should make you add to my collection as long as you kept it."

I sat up and asked him, "Man, why do you look at that stuff?"

"Have you seen those women? That's a stupid question."

"Come on, man, you know what I mean. You're a believer. No matter how tough you try to play, you want to please

God. Do you think He is alright with you getting off on this stuff?" I grabbed the magazine from underneath my mattress and gave it to him.

"For you to have held on to it for so long, don't think that I don't know you enjoyed it."

"Man, that's why I'm asking you, because it made me really aroused. I've just been thinking about it, just been fighting it. I just now believe that God wants more from my life than a head filled with filth. He wants me to get a girl and love her the right way, and to bring my troubles to Him and not to some magazine to release my tension. I'm sure I'm going to fall plenty of times before I am with Him, but I just want to be better. I just want to make Him proud. I'm going to do in His word. How will I know He will always be there for me if I never believe, if I never trust Him with the hard stuff? You and I are working on the hard stuff, Lance. You're my brother. You play football like nobody's business. I guess as I'm charging you, I'm charging us both to try to get it right for Him. Can we get better from our mistakes?"

He nodded, and walked away leaving me to pray that we really could be better.

"This just isn't working out between us."

I was just about to go into the player's lounge to watch Michigan take on Ohio State. I was excited that we were a couple again, but dang, I didn't want all of the drama. I told Lance and Deuce to go on in and I would see them in a second.

"So, what's all this about?"

"I just wanted you to be honest with me, that's all. Don't have me thinking you're this stellar guy when that's not the case."

"Savoy, what are you talking about?" I said, trying to keep my cool.

"Can we meet? Can we talk?" she asked, as if our very existence depended on it.

"Naw, I'm going to be with the guys. You know we're going to see who we play. You know this is an important game."

"Alright, fine then. Just forget it."

"Savoy, wait. Can we at least talk over the phone? What's going on?"

"Well, if you're over at the football complex, just ask Charlie."

"Ask her what? I just told you, I don't even want to talk to that girl. Savoy, baby, you got to be secure with us."

"And how is that at all possible if she showed me the stick?"

"I'm lost."

"Of a pregnancy test, which was positive."

"And what in the heck does that have to do with me?"

"She said it's yours. She said you were groggy and admitted a bunch of other stuff, but that day she came to your room . . ."

"Wait, just stop. Girl, you need to know that I don't need to lie to you. I want us to build something strong. Heck, we prayed. I got issues for real. I mean, so do you, but I know how bad I hurt you when I went back to my old high school girlfriend. I'm not going to jeopardize something with the girl I love with some girl who has been with half of my teammates. I mean, you're saying that I am the father. You need to check with your brother. That might be your niece or nephew is the word I heard."

"Well, why would she say that?"

"I don't know, but I know what I am trying to have with you. If you gonna be second-guessing me every time we turn around, then I can't do this."

Lance came rushing outside. "Man, you got to get in here. Michigan is getting whooped. We might have a chance, boy."

"Savoy, I got to go."

"So you just gonna get off the phone just like that?"

I was already overheated; it was like I was in a pot of water on high for ten minutes, boiling over. Why Charlie kept yanking her chain was something I couldn't understand, but something I couldn't keep reassuring her about either. This was my girl; I needed her to stay strong to keep me strong. I couldn't be a babysitter; I needed a companion. I simply said good-bye and hung up the phone, because whatever was going to be would be. When I walked into the locker room, all of my teammates that were there were screaming. When we lost to USC at the beginning of the year, it was close. Ohio State already had two losses, and they were killing Michigan. It wasn't like I didn't care about the game. It was just that, like everybody else in the room, I still wanted my chance at the national title. USC was ranked number one and we were number three. Michigan losing was our only way there. With all of the rankings and coaches' polls, they'd have to lose pretty bad. No one would have actually predicted that they would do that, but the game wasn't over. This was big, but equally important to me was what I had with Savoy.

While I watched the guys get down, I sat back and prayed: *I don't know, Lord. Even when I try to do the right thing with Savoy, our relationship ends up going wrong. I'm not trying to downplay who I am and the pressure that that may put on her as my girlfriend, but dang, there really are a lot of guys out here trying to use these girls. Here I am trying to do the right thing, and it just doesn't seem to be worth my trouble. Show me how to lead in a successful relationship, to give her the confidence that she needs, to make her know that I am accountable to You.*

Then the Chaplin came over and sat next to me. "You're heart ain't broken, is it? You look like somebody done killed your cat." God was good. He always knew what to give me when I needed it.

"I just don't have a strong relationship with this girl, that's all."

"Saxon's sister?" he asked, remembering. I nodded. "She's a good girl. Have y'all got into the word together? Have y'all gone to church together? Had any type of counseling for what the Lord expects out of your relationship?"

He could tell from my expression that the answers to all three of those questions were no.

"Well, why don't you start there. Start off by making sure the both of you have a great relationship with God, and the relationship between you two will come."

"She's just so insecure."

"Well, you still care about her. Anything worthwhile isn't going to be easy."

The final score was 22 to 10 Buckeyes.

Saxon came over to me and said, "Hey, my sister just called me crying." I didn't know what to expect from him next. "But I know you got it. So I just wanted to tell you that I know she's a little overdramatic. I think because it's her time of the month." Both of us had to chuckle. "But I meant what I said, you are good for her. I don't know if you want to talk to her, but she's in the library. I just wanted to let you know." We slapped hands and went our separate ways. Though Sax and I were different, maybe we would be able to coexist after all.

After I dropped Lance and Deuce off, I headed to the library. As I walked in, I hated that I didn't have a bunch of roses, but hopefully, the mere surprise of my presence would make the impact I wanted. I found her in a corner with her head buried in a book. She wasn't studying, she was reading a novel. I crept up behind her and she didn't even turn around. I covered her eyes, and bent down and kissed her ear and said, "Forgive your boyfriend for being a jerk?"

She stood up, turned around, and gave me a hug.

"No, it's me. It's this woman stuff that's got me over the top. You're right, I can't believe what everybody else says. Charlie and I have gone at it, and I don't know, I don't know."

"Well, I hope you still trust me."

"I do, Perry. You're a great boyfriend, and we have been off and on. How can I expect you to do anything?"

"No, I am talking about the spiritual part."

"That would be great," she said as she hugged me again.

Savoy and I were okay, so now I could put on my football cap again. Sunday at six, the whole team was in the meeting waiting to hear the bowl announcements.

Coach Red said, "Men, whether we get into the big game or not, I am proud of you. You guys worked hard this week. You have only one loss and are the ACC champs. Because you guys finally decided to jell, we're moving on. I'm extremely pleased to know you both individually and collectively."

When we didn't hear our names for any of the other bowl games, we began hollering. There was only one more to call. We were going to be playing in the bowl game in Miami.

"The Orange Bowl will be," the sportscaster said, "a rematch of this year's season opener—the Trojans and the Yellow Jackets."

Coach let the press come in and interview us individually. The mics were in my face, and they all asked the same question: How'd I feel about our bid?

"Personally, I'm excited about this game. I really took it hard that my performance was the main reason we lost to USC in the first place. So anyone who likes football needs to make sure they're with us at the beginning of next year, to see this rematch."

"You're player's point has gotten so much better, Perry," the reporter said, "What is the difference?"

With zeal and humility, I said, "Each week, I have learned to accept the person that I am, and none of us ever got the big head. We just worked as hard as we could. I think that when you learn to care about your teammates, as we have, and when you care about yourself enough to give your all, victory comes. We didn't know if we'd get into this game or not, but I'll tell you right now, it feels pretty great learning our fate."

Perry Skky Jr., Book 4:

# PRAYED UP

## Stephanie Perry Moore

### ABOUT THIS GUIDE

The following questions are intended to
enhance your group's reading of
PERRY SKKY JR.: PRAYED UP
by Stephanie Perry Moore

# DISCUSSION QUESTIONS

1. Perry Skky Jr. reflects on the last year of his life. Do you think he learned anything? Have you ever looked back on your past to try not to repeat mistakes?

2. Perry and Savoy take their relationship to the next level. Do you think they should have given in to temptation? What are ways you can get out of sticky dating situations?

3. Perry being unfocused is the main reason why the team lost their season opener. Do you think people were justified in being mad at him? How can you not let stress cloud your judgment?

4. Savoy thinks she is pregnant. Do you agree with how Perry responds? What would you do if you got terrible news?

5. Perry feels like he is letting God down. Do you think he has a right to be down? What are ways you can make sure you stay upbeat?

6. Perry finds out that his quarterback is betting on their games. Do you think Perry was wise to not report this information? How has God used you to help others get out of trouble?

7. Perry gets a porn magazine from Lance. Do you think he was right to be tempted by the pictures? How can you stay away from things that can ruin your mind?

8. Perry finds out that Deuce is failing classes and has drinking issues. Does he respond correctly by helping his friend? Can you remember a time when God al-

lowed you to help someone out of their bad circumstance?

9. Perry longs to have a stronger prayer life. Do you think Perry reaches his goal in this area? What are ways you can build your walk with God?

10. Perry and Savoy can't be apart. Do you think they can make it as a couple with all the obstacles in their way? How can two people strive to please the Lord in a dating relationship?

## Start Your Own Book Club

Courtesy of the PERRY SKKY JR. series

## ABOUT THIS GUIDE

The following is intended to help you get
the Book Club you've always wanted
up and running!
Enjoy!

## Start Your Own Book Club

A Book Club is not only a great way to make friends, but it is also a fun and safe environment for you to express your views and opinions on everything from fashion to teen pregnancy. A Teen Book Club can also become a forum or venue to air grievances and plan remedies for problems.

### The People

To start, all you need is yourself and at least one other person. There's no criteria for who this person or persons should be other than a desire to read and a commitment to read and discuss during a certain time frame.

### The Rules

People tend to disagree with each other, cut each other off when speaking, and take criticism personally. So, there should be some ground rules:

1. Do not attack people for their ideas or opinions.

2. When you disagree with a book club member on a point, disagree respectfully. This means that you do not denigrate another person for their ideas. There shouldn't be any name calling or saying, "That's stupid!" Instead, say, "I can respect your position, however, I feel differently."

3. Back up your opinions with concrete evidence, either from the book in question or life in general.

4. Allow everyone a turn to comment.

5. Do not cut a member off when the person is speaking. Respectfully wait your turn.

6. Critique only the idea (and do so responsibly; again, simply saying, "That's stupid!" is not allowed). Do not criticize the person.

7. Every member must agree to and abide by the ground rules.

Feel free to add any other ground rules you think might be necessary.

## The Meeting Place

Once you've decided on members, and agreed to the ground rules, you should decide on a place to meet. This could be the local library, the school library, your favorite restaurant, a bookstore, or a member's home. Remember, though, if you decide to hold your sessions at a member's home, the location should rotate to another member's home for the next session. It's also polite for guests to bring treats when attending a Book Club meeting at a member's home. If you choose to hold your meetings in a public place, always remember to ask the permission of the librarian or store manager. If you decide to hold your meetings in a local bookstore, ask the manager to post a flyer in the window announcing the Book Club to attract more members if you so desire.

## Timing is Everything

Teenagers of today are all much busier than teenagers of the past. You're probably thinking, "Between chorus rehearsals, the Drama Club, and oh yeah, my job, when will I ever have time to read another book that doesn't feature Romeo and Juliet!" Well, there's always time, if it's time well-planned and time planned ahead. You and your Book Club can decide to meet as often or as little as is appropriate for your bustling schedules. *Once a month* is a favorite option. *Sleepover Book Club* meetings—if you're open to excluding one gender—is also a favorite option. And in this day of high-tech, savvy teens, *Internet Discussion Groups* are also an appealing option. Just choose what's right for you!

Well, you've got the people, the ground rules, the place, and the time. All you need now is a book!

**The Book**

Choosing a book is the most fun. PRAYED UP is of course an excellent choice, and since it's part of a series, you won't soon run out of books to read and discuss. Your Book Club can also have comparative discussions as you compare the first book, PRIME CHOICE, to the second, PRESSING HARD, and so on.

But depending upon your reading appetite, you may want to veer outside of the Perry Skky Jr. series. That's okay. There are plenty of options, many of which you will be able to find under the Dafina Books for Young Readers Program in the coming months.

But don't be afraid to mix it up. Nonfiction is just as good as fiction and a fun way to learn about from where we came without just using a history text book. Science fiction and fantasy can be fun, too!

And always research the author. You might find the author has a website where you can post your Book Club's questions or comments. You can correspond with Stephanie Perry Moore by visiting her website, www.stephanieperrymoore.com. She can sit in on your meetings, either in person, or on the phone, and this can be a fun way to discuss the book as well!

## The Discussion

Every good Book Club discussion starts with questions. PRAYED UP, as will every book in the Perry Skky Jr. series, comes along with a Reading Group Guide for your convenience, though of course, it's fine to make up your own. Here are some sample questions to get started:

1. What's this book all about anyway?

2. Who are the characters? Do we like them? Do they remind us of real people?

3. Was the story interesting? Were real issues of concern to you examined?

4. Were there details that didn't quite work for you or ring true?

5. Did the author create a believable environment—one that you could visualize?

6. Was the ending satisfying?

7. Would you read another book from this author?

## Record Keeper

It's generally a good idea to have someone keep track of the books you read. Often libraries and schools will hold reading drives where you're rewarded for having read a certain number of books in a certain time period. Perhaps a pizza party awaits!

## Get Your Teachers and Parents Involved

Teachers and parents love it when kids get together and read. So involve your teachers and parents. Your Book Club may read a particular book where it would help to have an adult's perspective as part of the discussion. Teachers may also be able to include what you're doing as a Book Club in the classroom curriculum. That way books you love to read such as PRAYED UP can find a place in your classroom alongside the books you don't love to read as much.

## Resources

To find some new favorite writers, check out the following resources. Happy reading!

Young Adult Library Services Association
*http://www.ala.org/ala/yalsa/yalsa.htm*

Carnegie Library of Pittsburgh
Hip-Hop!
Teen Rap Titles
*http://www.carnegielibrary.org/teens/read/booklists/teenrap.html*

TeensPoint.org
What Teens Are Reading?
*http://www.teenspoint.org/reading_matters/book_list.asp?sort=5&list=274*

Teenreads.com
*http://www.teenreads.com/*

Sacramento Public Library
Fantasy Reading for Kids
*http://www.saclibrary.org/teens/fantasy.html*

Book Divas
*http://www.bookdivas.com/*

Meg Cabot Book Club
*http://www.megcabotbookclub.com/*

Stay tuned for the next book in this series,
PROMISE KEPT,
available May 2008 wherever books are sold.
Until then, satisfy your Perry Skky Jr. craving with
the following excerpt from the next installment.

ENJOY!

# ~ 1 ~
# Trying to Win

Okay, I couldn't believe that Savoy just slapped me. It was Christmas break and everyone was hanging out at Howard's barbeque. I was with my boys, Cole and Damarius, and some chicks were hanging around us, but I was being a good boy. I only had a few days 'til I had to head back to school and get ready to play in the National Championship college game.

After the slap, I didn't know how to feel. First of all, it hurt. So I was pissed. Second, my boys were just sitting there looking at me like they knew I wasn't going to take it. So I was angry.

Then I looked into Savoy's eyes. Through the tears that began to fall from her lashes, I could see she was hurting. So I felt bad. There was a little crowd of honeys watching and though I didn't want to be punked, something was going on with my girl.

"You two, don't even say anything to me!" I shouted to Damarius and Cole.

Damarius jerked me by the back of my shirt and said, "I know you ain't gone just let her talk to you like that."

"It's obvious that something is wrong with her. Can't you see? Come on, man. Give me some space," I said as I pulled away from Damarius.

"Aight, aight! Whatever, but you the one that's gonna miss out on all the fun," he said as he tapped Cole and they walked a few feet away.

Savoy just looked at me and wiped her face. I knew she was disappointed and for whatever reason she thought I had let her down. I could understand her being upset and all, but to come at me swinging and hitting me in public was unacceptable.

Her first semester in college must have been harder than I thought for her to lash out at me this way. Her bold gesture was dumb. We were working on rebuilding what we had after deciding to get back together. Just because I didn't play things her way she was pitching a fit, like some out-of-control toddler. I took a deep breath and motioned her to talk to me. After all, since she'd made such a bold stand to call me out, she certainly had something to say.

Savoy angrily snarled, "I can't believe you! You haven't talked to me in two days. And before that, you claimed you were *so* busy. Either you got to work out or you got to hang out with the guys. You've got to do something for your mom or dad. Shucks, you don't even have time for me. Then my brother gets me out of the house, and I find you flirting with a whole bunch of high school girls. You better be careful, or else you'll be in jail for child molest . . ."

"Okay, see, I've had enough," I told her quickly cutting her off. "Why are you being the over-jealous type?"

When she looked down, unable to respond, I figured maybe every girl had it in her. I could relate. I was certain that I didn't want to see her with another guy, but she shouldn't just assume that I was dissing her. I knew that no matter what I said, there was no way I was going to win. "So you can't answer me? You can't respond."

She shook her head. "Naw, I know you won't understand."

I said, "Try me. Say *something*. I don't appreciate you trying to humiliate me."

"You care more about what everybody else thinks instead of what I think."

"No, you don't respect me."

"Like you respect me," she said. "Please, Perry, if you did, you wouldn't lie to me. We'd be together. You'd make me a priority."

She just went on and on whining. It was so annoying. I had a lot of pressure on me. A lot of people were pulling me from all different kinds of directions. We said we were going to be an item, wasn't that enough for her?

"Just forget it, Perry. I don't even know why I try. I don't even know why I cared."

She went out of the restaurant. Like a nut, I followed her. I thought about my sister Payton. If there was one thing I had learned from her it was that during a certain time of the month girls went cuckoo. Maybe that was the case with Savoy, so I went over.

Gently, I stroked her soft brown hair. "So is it that time of the month for you or something?"

"Why does it have to be all of that? Can it be that I just want you to care? I don't understand why it's so hard for you to understand."

"You can't put limitations on me."

"I didn't."

"I'd think you'd understand that I haven't seen my friends or my family in practically months. With all that I have had to balance—from trying to be an A student to showing out on the field—it's just been one thing after another. Finally, I get the good news that I'm going to have the chance to play in the big game and I can't even celebrate." I sighed. "I mean, if you want to know everywhere I go, if you want to sign off on every little thing I do, then honestly this might be too much for me."

"Okay, forgetting me, putting me aside, Perry, could you honestly say that the Lord would be pleased at what you're doing right now? Don't you think that He would see your actions as a little suspect for a guy who is supposed to have a girlfriend?"

"Savoy, the Lord knows what's in my heart and I know He wouldn't condemn me because of something Damarius does. Yeah, he has five girls hanging on him, but they ain't hanging on me."

"Whatever, they are not around him because of him, everybody knows who you are. I've heard the buzz. Every girl in this barbeque wants you smothered between two slices of toasted bread. You've got 'potential millionaire' written all across your forehead. Are you stupid? Do you not see?" Savoy came at me worse than an attack dog.

Standing my ground, I said, "I told you I didn't want a jealous girlfriend." It was almost like she was about to hyperventilate, so I paused.

"Well, excuse me, but if you would be more of a boyfriend, and give me the same things that you expect from me, we wouldn't have these issues. And to answer your question from earlier, yes, I'm on my period right now. So I'm sorry for hitting you in public and all that. I wasn't trying to embarrass you. I was trying to get your attention; either you want to be in this relationship with me or you don't."

"Well, it can't be just your way. If you're saying those are the terms, then bye."

She turned around and threw her hands up in the air. Deep down I cared a lot about her. Way more then I ever did for Tori. I loved her, I just wanted to be cautious and keep my heart guarded. I wasn't trying to downplay all that she was saying, but I didn't see myself as all that either. Maybe God could help me check myself.

*Alright, Lord, if I'm wrong for having a little time for me, show me. If I'm supposed to be with Savoy, You need to show me how she and I can make it.*

Damarius and Cole walked up to me and Damarius said, "That's what I'm talking about. Let her walk away. You the man!"

Coach Red addressed the team in a frustrated tone. "Men, I'm disappointed in you. You've got to be self-motivated to make it to the top. No one can give you the desire to become the best. You've got a National Championship game to play and I know most of you went home for the full week I gave you off. Now most of you look like you haven't even worked out while away from our trainers and the facility."

There was talk that the coach had been going crazy. We knew it was stress from sportswriters speculating that another team should have gotten in the big game, not us. We heard we got voted in because of the politics coach played. He had a lot of pressure on him.

I didn't know why he thought we were unfocused, why he thought we didn't care. Just because we wanted to be around our family didn't mean that we weren't taking this seriously. I scanned the room and knew every player in there had the heart to win. Saxon raised his hand.

"Yes, Lee. What do you want?" Coach Red snapped.

"Coach, I just wanted to say that you told us we could go home. If that's not what you wanted, why'd you say it was alright?"

"I wanted you guys to make the decision to stay. When you're about to play in a big game, the biggest one you'll ever play in your life, you forgo some things. This National Championship game is *it*. You're getting a chance to play at the most outstanding level. I wanted my men to think. To be in the Championship game and to perform that night while millions are watching, you got to be on your toes. You got to be willing to sacrifice. If you say you want to win, you've got to give it your all," he said, shaking his head. "Yeah, I told you

you could go, but I didn't think you would. But I can't cry over spilt milk. Y'all are going to clean it up. Get out there and do a hundred suicides up and down the stadium steps."

We all grumbled.

"GET OUT THERE NOW!" he yelled.

Quickly, we fled out to the stadium. A line formed and we jogged the stairs. Of course, after twenty-five we were all tired.

"This proves my point. You guys didn't train hard enough this week. But that's okay because we're going to be ready for USC. Those Trojans are going to be ready for a war and we're going to give them one. Strap on your swords, bees, and let's lead 'em on to the hive," he said as our team got fired up.

Two days later, we were on a plane heading down to Miami. I had always heard that the Bowl games were something special, but to be in the biggest bowl was something special all in itself. And to play in it as a freshman, I truly was psyched.

As soon as we got there, the hotel's upscale lobby was swarming with press like we were celebrities or something.

Lenard came up to me with one of the other defensive guys and said, "Alright, bonding time."

"Just because we have the night off doesn't mean we need to go out on the town," I said, reminding them of the coach's philosophy. Just because an opportunity presents itself doesn't mean you have to seize it.

Lenard grabbed me by my collar and said, "Quit being a wimp. You're supposed to enjoy this time. You may have an opportunity to come back out here, but as seniors this is our last shot. We are up in the house and Miami here we come. You coming with us?"

"Yeah, I'm coming to keep y'all out of trouble," I said reluctantly. He was right—we wouldn't be here together like this again.

Unfortunately, the spot we chose was a bar full of Trojan fans. It wouldn't have been that big a deal, but Lenard was sporting his Jackets jersey. The crazy looks we got were eerie.

As soon as we ordered from the bar, a drunk bald guy yelled out, "The sorry Yellow Jackets are in the house."

I said, "Let's just go guys."

"Nah unh. I'm not about to leave without my drink," Lenard said.

I didn't have a good feeling, but what could I do? We sat down at a table, and tried to mind our own business and wait for the waitress to come and take our food orders. Then the same drunk fool came up to us with a few of his buddies and started a brawl.

He said, "I know you guys don't think you're going to win."

"Alright, man. Whatever. Nobody is mad that you're a Trojan's fan. Just get out of our face and we're cool." Lenard held up his hand in a peace sign.

Unfortunately, the guy didn't go away. "I know your new little freshman quarterback thinks he did good in the ACC Championship game, but we're gonna smash his head in. Who does he think he is? He's so stupid that he got himself ejected for betting on the games. Well, you better get ready to lose because your tired defense ain't much better. Shucks, you all shouldn't have even been playing in this game."

"Okay, I've had enough of him, y'all." Markus stood up and pushed the guy way back off into a corner.

It was on then, with everyone fighting from one end of the bar to another. At first I watched, but if I was anything, I was loyal. There were only a few of us, so my punches had to count. In no time, I heard sirens and folks started scattering.

I grabbed Lenard off of a man, then yanked on Markus. I shouted, "We've got to get out of here now!"

But before we could get away, the police herded us into a corner with the rest of the customers. I couldn't believe the

mess we were in. It didn't take law enforcement long to figure out who we were and haul us away. It seemed like an
even shorter time passed before an angry Coach Red showed
up at the precinct.

"Lenard! Perry! What is up with this? You've already been
suspended for fighting."

Lenard rushed to answer. "Folks started coming at us with
bottles and stuff. What are we supposed to do?"

Coach snarled, "You shouldn't have been out here in the
first place."

At the same time I was thinking, *Yeah, that's what I told
them.* But at that moment, what could I have done? I wasn't
strong enough to lead them to do the right thing. So I gave in
to the pressure and let them lead me into doing something that
was wrong. We had cuts on our faces, and Lenard was holding
his ribs. We had a National Championship game to play and
some of the key players were banged up over this foolishness.

Coach lectured us all the way back to the hotel. I heard
him, but he couldn't have made me feel more like a loser.

"It ain't like he's gonna bench us," Markus leaned over
and said as he clutched his stomach.

"You know what?" Coach said. "I heard that. All three of
you guys are going to sit out the first quarter of this game."

"You want to make that stupid move, Coach, then do what
you got to do," Lenard yelled back. What was he thinking?

Coach replied, "Since you're so big and bad, when you get
a chance to play, make up the difference. Fight on the field!"

Lenard lower his voice a few octaves and said, "But you're
tying our hands, Coach, by keeping us out one quarter."

Coach Red said, "What's fair is fair. Yes, I want to win a National Championship, but more than that, I want to make
you guys winners in life. Actions come with consequences.
Now you'll never forget how much your stupid actions cost
your team and your fans."